SMOKE AND MIRRORS

SMOKE AND MIRRORS

Lesley Choyce

A BOARDWALK BOOK
A MEMBER OF THE DUNDURN GROUP
TORONTO

Editor: Barry Jowett
Copy-Editor: Andrea Pruss
Design: Jennifer Scott
Printer: AGMV Marquis

Library and Archives Canada Cataloguing in Publication

Choyce, Lesley, 1951–

Smoke and mirrors / Lesley Choyce.

ISBN 1-55002-534-1

I. Title.

PS8555.H668S56 2004   jC813'.54   C2004-904889-9

1   2   3   4   5   08   07   06   05   04

 Conseil des Arts du Canada   Canada Council for the Arts   Canadä   ONTARIO ARTS COUNCIL CONSEIL DES ARTS DE L'ONTARIO

We acknowledge the support of the **Canada Council for the Arts** and the **Ontario Arts Council** for our publishing program. We also acknowledge the financial support of the **Government of Canada** through the **Book Publishing Industry Development Program** and **The Association for the Export of Canadian Books**, and the **Government of Ontario** through the **Ontario Book Publishers Tax Credit** program, and the **Ontario Media Development Corporation's Ontario Book Initiative**.

Printed and bound in Canada.
Printed on recycled paper.

www.dundurn.com

Dundurn Press
8 Market Street, Suite 200
Toronto, Ontario, Canada
M5E 1M6

Gazelle Book Services Limited
White Cross Mills
Hightown, Lancaster, England
LA1 4X5

Dundurn Press
2250 Military Road
Tonawanda NY
U.S.A. 14150

This book is dedicated to the memory of
Robyn MacKinnon

CHAPTER ONE

She first appeared in my History of Civilization class at 9:35 on a Thursday morning. Mr. Holman had long since given up on trying to entertain us. He had failed at being interesting and had retreated to the age-old teaching strategy of exerting as little energy as possible during class. Torpor, a kind of liquid dullness, had settled over the entire classroom like toxic haze as the teacher proceeded to simply read from the textbook.

We were lost in Babylon, on the Plain of Shinar to be specific. "The Plain of Shinar contained probably less than eight thousand miles of cultivable soil." Mr. H. had stumbled over the word *cultivable*, wondered if it was a legitimate word or not, and then asked for a show of hands from those who had heard anyone use the word before. Heavy eyelids and no raised hands throughout the room. "Hmm," Mr. H. pondered out loud, then proceeded.

"The Plain of Shinar was roughly equal in size to New Jersey or Wales." Hundreds of years passed as Mr. Holman continued to read. He himself yawned as he read of the early Sumerians on the Plain of Shinar. "Their settlements of low huts, at first of plaited reeds (wattle) and then of mud bricks, crept gradually northward, especially along the Euphrates, for the banks of the Tigris were too high for irrigation."

Davis Conroy was absent that day. He was three days into a false flu he had been cultivating to keep him home from school so he could play an ultra-violent video game called *Slayfest*. Through the window I could see the sun was out. This meant my father was playing golf. He took days off from work to play golf when the weather was good. He invited his favoured clients with him, so he considered golf part of his job. If the sun came out on the weekend, he played golf with other clients and called that work too. Even if he had promised his son that they would drive to the coast to watch the surfers. If the sun came out, it was golf and to hell with the surfers. To hell with promises to his son.

So in the midst of pondering the sunshine and cultivating my own viral anger, I blinked, and then suddenly she was there. She was sitting in Davis Conroy's seat. She was looking directly at me.

I must have appeared puzzled, because she waved her hand in front of my face then leaned towards me.

"Agriculture and cattle breeding produced most of the wealth which formed the basis of Sumerian life," she whispered.

"Agriculture and cattle breeding produced most of the wealth which formed the basis of Sumerian life," Mr. Holman echoed.

She smiled and put a finger to her lips. Then she held up one hand and touched her fingers and silently did a countdown. *Five, four, three, two, one.* The bell rang, and the rest of the class roused itself into mobility as the students began to collect books, scrape chairs, and spill out of the room. With a well-practised air of defeat, Mr. Holman closed up his volume of ancient history and, without looking up, gathered together what was left of his sad educational career and left the room.

When everyone was gone she cleared her throat and said, "You're Simon Brace, right?"

"I am. But you're not Davis Conroy."

"Davis Conroy is home with the flu. At least that's what he told his mother."

"You must be new."

"I am."

"I could have sworn that you weren't even there at the beginning of class."

"I knew it was going to be a very tedious class. So I missed the beginning of it."

She was attractive, yes, but not my dream girl. Not a Tanya Webb. Whoever she was, she was really messing with my head. I was absolutely certain she had materialized out of the blue.

"Out of thin air," she said, as if reading my thoughts.

"Oh crap," I said. "You can't read my thoughts, can you?" Given the weird crap that went through my head in the course of a day, I had a secret fear I would some-day meet someone who could look at my face and know what I was thinking.

"Not really. But I'm pretty good at estimating what a person is feeling, or if they are puzzled, I can quickly figure out what's puzzling them."

"You got a name?"

"Andrea."

"You're not from around here, are you?"

"Not exactly. I'm not enrolled here, if that's what you mean."

I studied her face, and she didn't seem to mind. She was prettier than I'd first thought. But I also saw some-thing sad about her. In her eyes.

"What do you see?"

"I see you."

"Do you think I'm attractive?"

"I didn't at first but then, well, yeah, I noticed."

"That's because I made you notice."

"You're doing some weird thing to me, aren't you?"

"No. Not that weird. I just made you notice."

"I'm thinking that I'm having some kind of mental episode. I've been reading a lot of books about metaphysical stuff. And I've been feeling stressed about a lot. My folks. This freaking school. My freaking life."

"That's why I'm here," she said. "Maybe I can help."

CHAPTER TWO

I am the product of two very ambitious parents. My father sells corporate bonds and my mother sells real estate. It seems there is no end to these two commodities. The hustling of houses and bonds goes on into the evenings and weekends by this man and his wife who more or less abandoned me, their son, many years ago. Abandoned is perhaps a harsh word, since I have a roof over my head, a refrigerator full of food, and most of the comforts desired by a young man of sixteen going on seventeen.

Despite the fact we all live in the same house, I think I've grieved over the loss of my parents for six or seven years now. I am an only child, and it's a good thing that my folks did not decide to bring another child into the world to be ignored by them.

I tried getting adolescent revenge on my parents in

several ways — poor grades, petty crimes, and household vandalism — but no matter how desperately I tried to bomb test after test, I'd end up with a C or C+. I could steal things from stores — CDs, gum, shoelaces, and running shoes even — and not get caught. I broke things around the house on purpose and they would be replaced without question.

Now my parents are hardly ever around to get mad at me. And they feel some guilt over not being around, so they buy me things. "If you have a problem, throw money at it until it goes away." My father said this about car trouble and problems with the furnace and the flying ant infestation. And I'm sure he applied the same solution to me. More money could always be made selling bonds to greedy investors on manicured putting greens.

My mother's favourite word in the English language is *closing*. "I'm *closing* on the Ferguson house today," she'd say in early morning glee at the breakfast table. "I bet I'll be *closing* on that condo by the end of the week." And so forth.

Ozzie Coleman had been my good friend since the third grade. In those days we were making evil-smelling concoctions we called fart bombs. I forget exactly what the famous combination was, but it was deep science to us, very serious business: filling plastic bags with our mix, leaving them in unlikely places where they would eventually be stepped on or ripped when a drawer opened, or sometimes just throwing them into crowds of unaware victims. No harm was done except for the stench, but the results were most gratifying.

Of course we went on to bigger and better adventures, and Ozzie was such a good friend that I never really cultivated any other friends.

Right after my accident Ozzie moved. His father moved him and his family because of some kind of corporate restructuring, I think. And I was left high and dry. We wrote letters to each other and talked on the phone, but it wasn't the same.

I became a loner after that. I had few social skills, and my parents tried to find a way to throw money at that problem, too. They couldn't buy me those skills, although they tried (and failed miserably) by enrolling me in kung fu classes, gymnastic programs, and even golf lessons. I told them I really wanted to learn to surf, but they laughed and said the ocean was two hours away. They weren't going to spend their Saturdays driving me to the beach. Besides, I might drown. It looked dangerous.

I trained myself at self-hypnosis by reading a book on the subject, and that helped some. I read about astral projection, and I found that pretty entertaining. And I began accumulating a great library of books (some stolen, some bought) on anything metaphysical.

I cut out clippings from newspapers and magazines about anything relating to the paranormal or anything that seemed inexplicable to the experts — survivors of freak accidents, weird weather phenomena, and UFO sightings, of course.

I wouldn't have called myself a happy camper by anyone's standards. But I was coping. Every once in a while I did something pretty weird, like walking around on the roof of our three-storey house with my eyes closed, or sitting outside on a full moon night waiting to be abducted by aliens I had tried to contact through mental telepathy. Otherwise, I traipsed through life one day at a time like all the other androids at my school.

Until everything changed that day when she appeared in my history class.

I was certain that she was real, but I had known for a long time that there is, for me at least, a pretty thin line between what is real and what is imagined. I am a believer in fuzzy lines of distinction of all sorts. What is alive and what is dead, for example. What is sentient and what is not. What is important and what isn't.

I realized that others my age didn't give a rat's ass about these trifles but were more intent on hockey, drugs, booze, or the interest of the opposite sex. Of this array of concerns, I admit that I had a strong lusting instinct when it came to certain female classmates, but I was inept in those necessary social skills. This may help explain why Andrea appeared to me.

We left the classroom together, and I decided to hold off on making any quick judgments. This was a skill learned in the scientific heyday of Ozzie and me — young researchers using pure scientific hypotheses in our attempts to create ever more noxious smells from household chemicals and cooking supplies.

Andrea carried herself gracefully, far more gracefully than most girls at Stockton High. I was afraid to touch her, and she kept teasing me about that.

"You think I'll disappear."

"You might."

"You think I'm not real?"

"I'm holding off on making that call."

We were in the hallway, and there were other students around. "Who are you talking to?" Kylie Evans asked when she saw me having what appeared to be a conversation with a fire extinguisher. What she would have heard me say then was, "You might," followed by "I'm holding off on making that call," two bits of conversation that may or may not make sense coming from a boy talking to safety equipment.

I wanted to say more to Andrea but decided to wait for privacy. I moved on down the hall oblivious to the usual rattle and chant of students changing classes. I was further oblivious as to where I was headed. Which classroom? What subject? What to do about Andrea? Suddenly there was a tug on my arm.

"You're going the wrong way," she said. "English is upstairs."

The hallway was thinning. I held my hand over my mouth when I spoke in hopes that no one would notice. "I could feel that. When you touched me."

"I seem to be corporeal in some respects."

"Seem to be what?"

"You felt my hand on your arm."

"I did."

The hallway was now empty. A very bright light was coming in through the glass doors at the end of the hall. It suddenly seemed like we were in a tunnel. I didn't like those implications at all.

"Oh crap."

"You keep saying that."

"This time I really mean it. I'm not ...?"

Andrea tugged at my arm again. Her smile was different this time — softer, sadder. "No, you're not. You are here in high school. You really are.

"I've always had a hard time distinguishing between death and school. In fact, it's one of my fears — that I'll die and wake up wherever you go to and I'll still be in school. Still listening to Mr. Holman drone on about the Sumerians."

"When the Sumerians died, they expected to need all their belongings in the next world." Andrea seemed inexplicably knowledgeable about ancient cultures. "They knew it was going to be a gloomy place under the earth with roots and dirt and worms, I guess. So they took along what they could. This included oxen and servants."

"How did they do that?"

"Those left behind killed them and piled up the bodies by the burial chamber."

"It must have been messy. How do you know this stuff, anyway?"

"I have no idea. But I do know they were wrong. The Sumerians didn't know squat about the afterlife."

"You're still freaking me out, you know."

"You need to get to English."

"And you?"

"I'll be there, but if there are no empty seats, I might just hover."

"You're kidding, right?"

"Try to keep an open mind. No labels. No judgments. First impressions are not always right."

"I know that," I said to the door and then turned the handle, apologized to Mrs. Dalway about being late, and went to take a seat in the back of the room.

Mrs. Dalway was launching an animated discussion about the witches in *Macbeth*. All the desks were filled with student bodies. Andrea walked to the side of the room and sat at one of the computers. She was typing on the keyboard, and I was sure others would notice. The computer's sound was off, but I saw images on the screen. I leaned hard backwards to see what she was doing, and it seemed that she was checking her email.

Mrs. Dalway picked up her voluminous volume of Shakespeare and, with great authority, read the lines of a character she called "Witch Number Two":

> Fillet of fenny snake,
> In the cauldron boil and bake;
> Eye of newt and toe of frog,
> Wool of bat and tongue of dog,
> Adder's fork and blind-worm's string,
> Lizard's leg and howlet's wing,
> For charm of pow'rful trouble,
> Like a hell-broth boil and bubble.

CHAPTER THREE

When I was twelve I had a skateboarding accident. My father had this assessment of my skateboarding style: "Simon, you are reckless and lacking any semblance of good judgment." He probably said this because I was reckless and lacking any semblance of good judgment. But I had not yet learned to practise astral projection, so I was using a skateboard to expand my boundaries of possibilities.

My parents were already busy professional people at this point in my life — heck, they had been like that since I was in diapers. In fact, I think, my birth was an accident, I was an accident, and perhaps that accident-mode was following me as I grew up. Most of us do not like to admit that there are parents in the world who probably should not have been parents, but I think you could apply this to mine. They were born for real estate and corporate bonds. They had no great commitment to perpetuate the species or to raise me. They lavished money on babysitters, and as a result I had some of the best and some of the worst.

It was a babysitting wonderland until about eleven, and by then I was good and pissed off at my parents for trying so hard to ignore my existence. I don't know what form of wisdom had kicked in, but they were wise enough not to have a second child. I expect they believed, by this point, that their first one was a bit of a failure or at least a freak (with his fart bombs, his comic books, his interest in the paranormal, and his pitiful grades at school).

The skateboard was a fantasy tool for me. Ozzie (short for Osmond) was still part of my life in those days and as good as it got when it came to having a loyal but weird friend for a weird kid. My parents never said much to Oz because they didn't like him. They said he had a funny smell — it was the foreign cheeses he ate with much gusto. They said he was a bad influence — he had introduced me to cracking my knuckles and skateboarding. They said I should get other friends.

Pretty much all of my friends up to that point had been imaginary. Or as I explained it, they existed on an alternate plane of existence. Which didn't mean they weren't real; they just weren't *here*.

Oz showed me videos of young, fearless kids not much older than us doing death-defying feats, and I knew I could do those things. I wanted to fly on my skateboard. It was inconceivable that I could be injured.

We started out on steep streets racing straight down the white line towards ill-placed stop signs. No slalom, no turns at all, just straight cowabunga-screaming gravity-fed speed. I liked the way the wind felt in my hair and the sound it made in my ears. I used my mental powers (the ones I refused to activate in school) to will traffic to let me slide across the intersection and up the driveway of the house situated there. Sometimes there were car horns heralding my triumph, sometimes skidding tires and shouts of appreciation or rage.

I always found a lawn or at least a flowerbed to end my spree. I was that good. I was gold.

By the age of twelve, I had the baggy clothing and an array of scars. I had experienced road rash on nearly every inch of my body. I had a nasty attitude towards anyone who looked at me funny when I was in skater mode. Oz had somehow sobered himself up into being more cautious, but I was an adrenalin junkie who didn't mind kissing asphalt if that was what it took.

I was a railing artist. I skidded down metal railings wherever I could find them. I didn't care what was at the bottom. Usually just concrete. I understood that concrete was hard and flat and unforgiving but I'd made my peace with that. Oz said I understood the physical nature of concrete — up close and personal —

more than any other person on this planet or any other planet in the solar system. Oz had taken a backseat in the thrill-and-spill-a-minute world of skateboarding. He had introduced me into the lifestyle and then sat back, nursing his small wounds and watching me go for the glory. He was my number one (and only) fan.

My mother insisted I get professional help for my "problem" (and this was not the first time for that). But it turned out that the professional help was on my side. "He's just trying to get your attention," Dr. Rickbenbacker told my parents. "You need to spend a little more time with your son." Grumbling and griping the whole way about a golf game missed and potential bond business down the tubes, my father took me fishing. I wasn't really interested in fishing. "Let's go to the beach," I begged. "I want to learn to surf."

"We're going fishing," he said, gritting his teeth, gripping the steering wheel tightly as he beheld visions of corporate bonds, whole truckloads of them, being sold to unwary investors by his rabid competitor, Hal Gorey.

Turned out there was a cell phone in the glove compartment, and it rang. It rang often. The fish were not biting at the fish farm he took me to. We bought a salmon, already cleaned and filleted, as evidence of father-son bonding.

Just for the record, let me say that I was not trying to kill myself. It's safe to say, though, that skateboarding had consumed me. If there had been an ocean handy, I would have been surfing and falling off into salt water. But I had no ocean, only streets and sidewalks and elaborate steps to public buildings and railings and ornaments of various shapes and sizes. What I had to fall onto was concrete or asphalt. It was not my destination of choice, but it was what was available when I was ready to fall.

I would be lying if I told you that I did not enjoy coming home with a bloody nose, a forehead abrasion, or a nicely mangled knee. These were all showy awards for attempting the impossible. A kid trying to liberate himself from various laws of physics and reality wants to show off his effort, if not his success.

Ozzie had a bad habit of locating new venues for me to try — places he himself would not attempt. Twice he suggested the long, three-tiered set of granite steps in front of the downtown courthouse. Better yet, there was the metal railing going down the middle.

It was an in-service day for teachers, the sort of day when kids have no classes and go for broke with parents away at work. Teachers were cloistered away in meeting rooms gossiping about their students and inventing new ways to bore them to tears. Meanwhile, Oz and I would rule downtown. We were twelve and had the right clothes, the right skateboards, and enough attitude to start a world war.

The steps were impressive, and the railing gleamed in the sun. We ran up the steps and, without even a split second to determine where I might end up, I placed my board with me atop it on the railing and began my descent. It was another cowabunga moment with adults aghast, pulling their hands off the railing as I slid south at the speed of infinity. I stayed focused, kept my wits about me, and was near the bottom when something went wrong. My board caught on metal, and I was launched into the air.

All of the arguments about safety helmets had fallen on my two deaf ears, of course, and some protective Styrofoam would have come in handy at the moment my skull made impact with the curb. A bus tire skidded to a stop a full twenty centimetres before crushing my skull, but my head had come down hard on that darned curb. I was delivered into unconsciousness and went someplace else while pedestrians tried to figure out what to do with my unconscious body. Ozzie began to cry. He thought he had killed me. He kept shouting, "It isn't fair" for some reason, but I guess he thought I was a goner and that my life had been too short.

Someone would later explain that my brain had been bruised (along with my ego) and that it was a pretty serious concussion as far as concussions go. I did not die and then resurrect like a Jesus Christ of skateboarders or any-thing. But I did travel to someplace far from Stockton.

It was a beach, I can tell you that. And everything was shimmering (a word Mrs. Dalway says is over-used). And there were two beautiful girls. (I'm sorry, but there were.) They were wonderful and sweet and they were surrounded by light. Everything was fuzzy in an extremely bright sort of way. I thought I recog-nized them both as my two all-time favourite babysit-ters, but I could not make out their faces very well. I just knew that I was someplace safe and happy. A young man with a surfboard walked up to me and held out something in his hand. I put out my own hand, palm upward, and he dropped into it twenty or so of those little shiny ball bearings used in skateboard wheels. He motioned up at the sky, and I seemed to understand that I was supposed to throw the ball bear-ings up, so I did.

The little steel balls flew to the sky and hovered there, each becoming a small, beautiful planet. Everyone on the beach applauded.

I don't want to sound melodramatic, but it was like the first time in my life I felt truly appreciated. I felt loved. And I did not want to have to return to my old, ordinary self.

But I eventually returned anyway — to a blinding headache and a hospital room with a TV. *The Simpsons* was on, and Homer was trying to save the nuclear power plant from a meltdown.

And I remember my mother crying one time when she came into my room and thought I was asleep. I recall feeling her tears soak through my hospital gown. She said that she loved me very much and if I would only get well, she would promise to be a better mother. When I did start to get better, though, she didn't show the same kind of affection. But both of my parents seemed relieved that I was back.

I recall one doctor, too; I think he was still in medical school, and he had kind of long blond hair and a really relaxed way of talking to me. He was a *Star Trek* fan too and used to quiz me about Klingons and Star Fleet regulations. I remember that. He played chess as well, but poorly. No sense of strategy at all, and he was easy to beat.

All the time I was in that hospital room, I never felt alone. I had my own room — my father saw to that, big spender that he was in those days. Doctors came and went. Orderlies, nurses. But there was something else as well, like a presence of some sort, like someone was watching over me, making sure I was okay, even when no one was in the room.

By the time I left the hospital, I had regained most of my memory, but it had holes in it. I couldn't remember if I liked Coke or Pepsi better. I couldn't remember which channel *Star Trek* was on. Or which drawer in the kitchen had the knives, forks, and spoons.

They said I suffered some short-term memory loss, which came in handy as an excuse for doing so poorly on a math test and French vocabulary quiz (both of which I had never studied for). My parents gave me only a short, incomprehensible lecture about how foolish I had been. They bought me things to make me feel better, but my father threw away my skateboard, which the ambulance driver had kindly returned to my house after the accident.

The doctor explained my lethargy as part of post-traumatic stress. "His accident," he said, "has had as much of an emotional impact on him as if he had been in a war." I did continue to have that image of the bus floating towards me the split second before I was knocked out. But that wasn't what was bugging me. I really wanted to get back to that beach and those people on it. My old babysitters and the surf dude who handed me the tiny ball bearing planets.

Regular life just wasn't going to work for me anymore.

CHAPTER FOUR

I accidentally started to pay attention to Mrs. Dalway, who was telling us she had once seen Mel Gibson acting in a live version of *Macbeth*, and I was wondering why he would want to do a thing like that. I had liked Mel Gibson in the movie *Braveheart*, and when I was thirteen, he had me thinking of taking up sword fighting as a lifelong career until it clicked in my still slightly bruised brain that there probably wasn't much of a calling for sword fighting anymore.

Then Mrs. Dalway read a few more lines from the bard:

> Who can impress the forest, bid
> the tree
> Unfix his earthbound root? Sweet
> bodements! Good!

Such was my distraction that I had not been keeping an eye on Andrea, and when I looked over towards the computers she was gone.

What I did next was considered to be quite unusual in a high school English classroom. I began to cry. I really did.

I know. A sixteen-year-old boy crying in the middle of Shakespeare is a little weird — well, a lot weird. I mean, almost anyone at Stockton High could tell you I was not normal. Normal and me just didn't go hand in hand. It wasn't the first time I'd cried. I'd done it before. And it's not just a sudden downpour of tears. It's not like throwing up where it just suddenly happens when you eat some bad pizza.

My crying is attached to a very deep-seated emotional response to things. I can't watch the news, for example. If bombs are dropping or if children are starving or even if the president of the United States is spreading hatred again with one of those speeches — well, I'll start to blubber.

Mrs. Dalway thought I was so moved by her reading that it had unleashed the floods. She stopped midspeech, looked my way, and seemed stunned. She had never moved a student to tears before.

"Are you all right?"

I blew my nose loudly. "I'm okay. Continue," I said, droopy-faced and sodden.

The class was laughing by now. What else could they do? Many of them had seen me act oddly before, but I was still a reliable source of entertainment. Mrs. Dalway stumbled over her lines and finally gave up. "Are there any questions?" she asked. The old standby.

Tanya Webb, a girl whose beauty had held my attention for quite a long time, raised her hand. "Is any of this going to be on the exam?" This was the question she asked in every class.

Mrs. Dalway set her book down on her desk and just stared at Tanya. Then, in a bit of a fluster, she asked us to spend the rest of the class writing down our impressions of Macbeth as a person and what advice we would give him if he were our best friend. Eventually the bell rang and feet began shuffling out of the room.

I handed in a blank sheet of paper with my name on it. I was sorely afraid that this amazing girl, Andrea, real or imagined, had swept into my life for a brief encounter and then disappeared forever. I had not figured out who she was or even what she was, but I was certain she was the best thing that had happened to me in a long, long time.

"Simon, are you sure you are all right?" Mrs. Dalway asked.

I wasn't all right. My world had collapsed around me like a bubble yet again and I was adrift in a meaningless universe, but all I said was, "I'll be okay."

The upside was that Mrs. Dalway would probably take pity on me — or secretly be pleased that I seemed to be so moved by her Mel Gibson story and the reading — and would give me a good grade no matter how badly I screwed up. And when it came to school, I screwed up badly and often. So there was this positive aspect.

But aside from that glimmer of academic brightness, I was devastated. Over the years my parents had invested heavily in the proper professional treatment to see if something could be done about my emotional outbursts. Although they disagreed about a lot of things during what little time they spent at home, they were unanimous in wishing they had produced a normal child instead of me.

The skateboard near-death head injury had supposedly severed some of the connective tissue between the left hemisphere and right hemisphere of my brain. One doctor had even shown me a model of the brain in its two lovely halves. I held one half in my hand; Dr. Yumato held the other half in his. "See," he said, "two seemingly independent parts of the brain. Now give me back the left hemisphere."

He wanted to prove some point about how the two were normally connected but, because I was annoyed by his condescending attitude, I would not hand back to him the left hemisphere of the brain. "This is not a game," he said.

But it was a game. It was all a game. I didn't like what he was telling me about my connective tissue and I didn't like the way he was treating me like a child. I was nearly thirteen at that point. Dr. Yumato became angry with me. "You are a very stubborn boy," he said. This was not news to me. "You cannot be helped if you keep acting like this."

Maybe that's why I kept acting like that. I don't know, but I never did give him back his other half of the brain. It's still in my room at home and it is one of my prized possessions.

The doctors all agreed I could not have my two hemispheres stitched back together. There was no quick fix, no easy repair. Most thought I would just have to adapt. So I would remain a kid and ultimately a teenager with some problems. Emotional. Mental. But adapting as best as I could with my two free-floating hemispheres in my head.

My parents were continually disappointed that they couldn't buy their way back to having a normal son. Sometimes they argued with each other about whether I had been normal even before the clunk on the concrete. Sometimes I cried myself to sleep at night listening to them through the wall. At such times, I wished myself back on that beach I had been on with the two girls and the surfer pouring the ball bearing planets into my hands. Other times I wished I were dead.

After my teary English class, a fight broke out between Charles Fishman and Barry Sung. It was one of those odd high school disagreements between two ethnically proud individuals. Fishman was Jewish and Sung was Chinese and they were arguing over who made better hockey players, Jews or Chinese. It's possible that this argument had never happened before anywhere on earth, but that's the way our high school was. I wasn't going to be the one to break it up. I had my own problems with my right brain probably not even knowing what my left brain was doing. I wondered if I would eventually grow up to have a split personality and end up having my own arguments with myself as to who were better hockey players, left-brained people or right-brained people.

Tanya Webb looked right at me as I walked to my locker. I had known Tanya since the second grade, and while I had evolved into this strange creature that I now was, she had somehow matured into a beautiful and sometimes intelligent young woman. She had a legion of male admirers and I was at the far perimeter of that crowd, but she was not an insensitive goddess. And today, in post-English-class-meltdown, she took pity on me, I suppose, and walked alongside of me down the hall.

"You really like Shakespeare, don't you?"

"It's the beauty of the language," I lied.

"I know what you mean. It's fluid and musical."

"And all those deep meanings," I added.

"What do you think she'll ask on the exam?"

Well, that was a bit of a letdown. I didn't care. I wasn't going to study for the exam. I never did. "I don't know," I said. "But maybe we can study together or something?"

In high school, we always added vague phrases like "or something" into our conversations just to open up opportunities. My seemingly innocent proposal was pretty far out on a limb for me, but my crying jag had left me feeling reckless and, having lost my imaginary friend Andrea, I was going for broke.

Tanya looked down and seemed to be studying the trash on the hallway floor. "I'm sorry, I don't think I can," she said, letting me down as gently, I guess, as she could.

"Maybe the exam will be easy anyway," I said.

Tanya smiled what I'd call a one-quarter smile and fled down the hall, swallowed by the crowd of noisy end-of-the-school-day students.

Amazingly, Andrea was there at my locker when I arrived. She had been watching me talk to Tanya. I felt a wave of euphoria sweep over me. She was back.

"I was afraid you were gone. One minute you were at the computer and then gone the next."

"You'll have to get used to me coming and going."

"I was afraid it was like some kind of computer virus had sucked you into cyber world or something."

"I'm not computer generated, if that is on your list of theories."

"That's comforting. But I still have a long list."

"Willing to share the top five?"

"Well, the top one is currently that you don't exist at all. That you are a product of my own mental imbalance."

"I hadn't noticed you were imbalanced."

"I cried when I thought you were gone. I mean, I really let go. Would a balanced person have done that?"

"I'm touched."

"Maybe you should tell me why you're here."

"I have some theories too, but I really don't know the whole truth. I just know I'm supposed to be with you."

Sung and Fishman had apparently made up and they were walking by me now, best of friends. They must have thought I was talking to them because they turned and stopped. I just waved. "Gonna watch the game tonight on TV?" I asked.

"Wouldn't miss it," Sung said.

They did not see Andrea. "Am I the only one who can see you?" I asked her after Sung and Fishman had moved on.

"So far, just you. Which is what makes me think I am here to do something for you. *Help* you in some way. But that's just a hypothesis."

"Do you have any special powers?"

Andrea looked straight at Lisa DeLong, another one of the students who had seen me cry in English, walking towards us carrying an armful of textbooks. Suddenly Lisa dropped a pencil, stopped, and picked it up, almost spilling her books.

As Lisa walked by, she paused and smiled. "See you tomorrow, Simon."

"Bye, Lisa." And she walked on.

"What about that?" Andrea asked.

"That what?"

"The way she smiled at you."

"You're saying you made her do that?"

"When was the last time she even gave you the time of day?"

"I'm not totally without my charms."

"You wanted to know about my 'special powers.' Well, I'm just beginning to figure out what I can and cannot do. I don't know how special they have to be to impress you, but I made her look at you. And I made her feel something, some small thing, something warm and fuzzy towards you just then."

"Oh," I said. "Like mind control?"

"No, Simon. All I can do is tweak a person's emotions. I can't change what they will do. I can't totally change the way they feel. But if someone is feeling angry I can make them angrier. If they are feeling kind, I can make them a little kinder."

"So you *tweaked* Lisa DeLong's feelings towards me?"

"Just then. Just a little."

I was beginning to see some possibilities here.

"How am I feeling right now?" I asked.

"You seem to be feeling pretty good."

"So do something with that."

And damn. I suddenly felt a little better. A bit lighter. The weight of this crazy world had been lifted from my shoulders.

Andrea smiled at me. My own elevated spirits seemed to have lifted hers as well.

"So there has to be a bit of mind reading involved here, yes?"

"I suppose so. You might call it that. It's just that I know certain things. I don't know where the information comes from. In fact, there's an awful lot I don't know, so you'll have to bear with me as I figure things out."

I was still smiling, still on my emotionally tweaked little buzz of being happy. I took hold of my padlock and was going to turn the numbers when I stopped.

"What's the combination?" I asked her.

"That's easy. Right to twelve, left to thirty-seven, right to twenty-one." She was totally certain she was right. She worked the combination herself, but the lock would not open.

She was one hundred percent wrong. "Sorry," I said, and cranked back and forth on the dial until the lock snapped open.

Andrea suddenly looked distraught. She was staring at the lock, and I felt like there was a great distance between us. I tried to say something reassuring but couldn't find the right words.

Then she seemed to remember something. "Of course," she said. "That couldn't be your combination. It belongs to someone else."

"Who?"

"Never mind," she said. "It's not important."

CHAPTER FIVE

A ndrea told me to forget about the bus. She wanted to walk.

"You're going to come home with me?"

"You thought I wanted to stay here at school?"

"My parents are going to love this."

"Just pretend I'm not there."

Andrea wanted to walk the old abandoned railway hiking path that follows the river. I'm not sure how she knew about it. Out of the blue she started naming trees and birds. "Oak, chokecherry, tamarack, alder, hemlock, maple. Goldfinch, purple martin, grackle, blue jay, mourning dove."

It was beautiful walking through the forest like this. I almost never went hiking. I would take the bus home, and my brain would whirr, but I usually talked to no one. I would arrive to an empty house, my dutiful parents still hustling their bonds or houses somewhere else. I had no dog, although I had always wanted a dog. I had a computer program of a dog that my father bought me. When I turned on my computer, it barked and wagged its cybernetic tail on the screen, and I would open a door by clicking the mouse and let it "out" where it barked some more and peed on an imaginary lawn. Sometimes there would be the voice of an angry neighbour yelling at my dog. The dog was not real, so I never gave it a name. Just called it "the dog."

"How did you learn all the names?" I asked Andrea.

"I don't know. I seem to have a selective memory. This place, this trail, this forest. It is familiar. I've been here before."

"Like in another life?"

"Do you believe in reincarnation?" she asked.

I stopped and leaned against what I thought was an oak tree. "I'm the guy who believes in everything. When I was younger, my friend Ozzie told me I could fly, so I believed him and I jumped off the garage roof. I flew for a second or two and then hit the ground, but it never occurred to me then that I couldn't fly. It would just take a little more practice. The Buddhists and Hindus believe in reincarnation, and I've never met a Buddhist or Hindu I couldn't trust. If it is metaphysical, I believe in it. But I don't think *you* were reincarnated suddenly as a seven-teen-year-old girl. I don't think it works that way."

"You think I am seventeen?"

"Am I wrong?"

"I'm sixteen," Andrea said, but as she said it she seemed to remember something.

"What are you thinking about?"

She shook her head, pointed to a tree with red berries. "Mountain ash. Also known as a rowan tree. Said to have magical powers."

"Trees are great, aren't they? Big, heavy-duty photosynthesis machines. When I grow up I want to be a tree."

Andrea laughed. She laughed very loudly for a girl of sixteen. "I haven't laughed like that for a long time."

"How long?"

"That I don't know. Let's stop."

We sat down by the river, and I stared into the water. First I saw the water moving, then the stuff on the surface — dust and twigs and a few leaves. Then I saw us. Both of us quite clearly. I looked different. Older maybe. A tad less insane looking around the eyes. No one ever came out and said I looked crazy, but I knew that some people thought so. Not Charles Manson crazy, just harmless crazy. In the river I didn't look crazy. It was like I was watching a movie of a different me — a guy and a girl sitting by a moving river in a world of trees and birds.

And then all of the birds suddenly stopped singing. The image in the river grew fuzzy like a TV with bad reception. It was from a breeze that had come up, stirring the surface of the water. There were clouds now as well — not clouds that said, *We're going to unleash buckets of rain on you and make thunder and hit you with a thirty-thousand-volt thunderbolt.* Just clouds.

I was wondering if she somehow did that — made the birds stop singing and the wind start up to erase my movie. And the clouds.

"It wasn't me," she said.

"You're reading my mind."

"No. Not really. You gave me a look, and I answered the look."

Because of the change of lighting Andrea looked different. Very pale. Some famous director once said that in movies, lighting is everything. Sometimes this can be applied to real life too. My mind jumped to the conclusion that Andrea was fading, maybe vaporizing in front of me. I didn't want her to leave, so I reached out to touch her arm.

I touched the cloth of her sleeve. It was cotton, and I slid my hand down until I was touching her wrist. The smoothness of the skin over her wrist left a powerful impression that will last the rest of my days. Then I put my thumb in the centre of her palm, my fingers on her knuckles, and I squeezed a little.

"You're testing me again to see if I'm real, aren't you?"

I felt a little silly. "Let's walk. I'm really glad you brought me here."

"For me there's a sort of déjà vu feel to it."

"I'm the world's biggest fan of the déjà vu," I said. "I've kept a list of them, at least the ones since I was in the hospital when I was twelve. They don't seem to make any sense at all, but I'm hoping that someday they will. Usually it's trivial stuff. I'm doing my homework and the lead breaks on my pencil. Wham. Déjà vu. I'm sitting down to toast at breakfast, open up a jar of raspberry jelly, and there it is again. You don't think it's one big, long, repetitive loop we live over and over and these are just snippets of things that sneak through into our current memory?"

"Where did you get that idea from?"

"*Star Trek*. I've logged a lot of hours on the Starship *Enterprise*."

"My brother used to ..." she stopped and had that distant, puzzled look again.

"Your brother used to what?"

"Watch *Star Trek*."

"You have a brother?"

"I think so," she said. "I remember him, or at least something about him, but it isn't clear at all. I'm not sure I can tell you more."

"And so the mystery deepens."

Now she seemed a little defensive. "Remember, this isn't about me. It's about you. I'm here to help you."

I smiled. "And believe me, I can use all the help I can get, so if I ask you anything you don't want to answer or say anything stupid, just ignore it and go on about your business of helping me."

But the inquiring mind is a devilish tool, and I did continue to ask her questions about trivial things in hopes of getting an inkling of who exactly it was that was trying to help me. I asked her several easy questions about *Star Trek* shows, but she didn't seem to remember anything. But then it was her "brother" who had been the fan, not her. And I began to wonder if she meant brother literally or if it referred to someone like her — another apparition or spirit or even this, the word that I did not want to test on her: *ghost*.

When we arrived at my house I was feeling a little dizzy — not surprising, I wasn't in great physical shape. I hadn't exercised much, and I loathed most sports that didn't require surfboard wax or ball bearings. Since mentioning her brother, Andrea had taken a couple of mood swings, and I tried to cheer her up with recitations of all the trivia in my head.

"The man who invented chop suey was Li Hung-chang. The father of frozen foods was Clarence

Birdseye. Milton Loeb invented the Brillo pad, and Francis Davis invented power steering." Then I explained to her about my severed hemispheres. "The doctors don't have a clue if they have reconnected in any way, but my 'problem' seems to allow me to memorize vast quantities of seemingly useless information."

"Do you still think that I may be something conjured up by your imagination?"

"My definition of what is real is anything I believe in. And right now, I believe in you more than I believe in the existence of God or McDonald's or that Jeep Cherokee coming down the street."

"Good. Although I think you might do well not to speak about me to anyone."

"Like my parents?"

"Especially them."

We were at my front door. I took the key out from under the mat and opened the door, then punched the code on the security system so it wouldn't go off. "Be it ever so humble," I said and invited Andrea in, but she seemed frozen on the front steps.

"I can't go in. Sorry."

"Why?"

"I'm not sure. But I just have a feeling that I shouldn't be in your house. It's almost like I'm not allowed."

"Where will you go?"

"Don't worry. I'll be around. I'm not really going anywhere."

"I don't want to lose you."

"It's okay," she said, touched my hand once, and began to walk away.

I assumed that Andrea's not wanting to come into the house had something to do with my parents. If buildings absorb negativity then my house had absorbed its share. Andrea was sensitive in this area. She had told me school had an odd balance of positive and negative that didn't "overload" her emotions.

A sixteen-year-old should probably never try to describe his own parents, but this one will do that anyway.

My mother must have been a knockout when she was young — in fact, I can tell that men still find her attractive. She uses her good looks and flattery of the male species to sell houses. I find this appalling, but then this is my mother. The woman has smarts but hides them sometimes, which I think makes her conniving.

My father was class president in high school and valedictorian at the university he went to. He was an achiever and always wanted to be the best. He married my mom because she was this great-looking woman. While others of his generation set about trying to save the world, my father set out to make a lot of money. What he actually does each day is a bit of a mystery to me, but it involves persuading big-time investors to invest in corporate bonds. He's explained to me what a corporate bond is but it doesn't really make any sense. A company that already has a huge amount of money borrows from another company, or a wealthy investor, more money to do something that will make them all more money.

Dad was a high flyer in this circus until some of those corporations went bankrupt and his bond buyers lost big bucks. So poor old Dad had to step down several rungs on his corporate ladder.

Both Mom and Dad had decided not to have any children but to dedicate their lives to the worthy cause of capitalism, but I came along, prompting my father to give up faith in various birth control methods and have a vasectomy, which he often speaks of in public.

As previously noted, I was a peculiar child, although no one could pin me down with a label. Attention deficit disorder, maybe. Hyper attention deficit disorder. Other terms were applied. My loving parents fed me Ritalin for a couple of years, and the teachers noted how my behaviour had improved.

I kept trying to fly — jumping from trees and roofs and second-storey windows. Skateboarding took me to the next level, and Ozzie was my coach. After the accident, I was a little stranger to the world, but I felt just fine after the headaches went away.

I didn't have friends like most kids, and a lot of the kids I knew, if given the chance, found ways to make fun of me. I was more interested in the paranormal than the normal anyway. So once Ozzie had moved, I was pretty much on my own, trying to bend spoons with my mind, travel by astral projection, or devise ways to make contact with those aliens that I was sure were watching over us.

Periodically, a teacher or a school principal would report my odd behaviour to my parents, who had long since given up on their dream of having a normal, possibly even a high-achieving, son. I know I was a disappointment to them. Once there was discussion with medical experts about reconnecting the right and left hemispheres of my brain more effectively, but the doctors concluded that it couldn't be done.

In truth, I was glad I was not normal. Normal seemed dull. Predictable. In my curious universe, all manner of entertaining surprises happened. Which is why I stopped taking my pills, my meds, as my mother called them, quite a while ago. My parents thought I was taking them. Certainly the drugstore was paid handsomely for the prescription. Clearly the doctor had made notes about how effectively the medication was working on his patient.

Often, as often as possible perhaps, my parents chose to leave me alone. They had little interest in the things I was interested in. They thought extra-sensory perception was a lot of hogwash. Even if my father believed ESP existed then he probably would have used it to persuade clients to buy his bonds.

One of my favourite ESP games was to look at someone who was not looking at me. Anyone. A guy in a mall. A girl in class. Seven times out of ten, if you looked long enough, the other person sensed someone looking at them and turned to look at you.

My mother wished I would stop going out on the lawn at night with my telescope to look for UFOs. The neighbours thought I was spying on them, but I had little interest in my neighbours. I saw things in the sky that might have been UFOs, and I would try to send the aliens in the spacecraft telepathic messages like, "If you receive this, please bring me ice cream so that I know you can hear me."

But not once did an alien with ice cream show up at my house.

My parents, I'm sad to say, were in a kind of competition with each other over who was the most successful at their work. I think my mother was slightly ahead of my father, and this was not good at all for the male ego. I don't know why they were so caught up in their jobs, and they couldn't understand why I didn't have more interest (or respect) for what they did. I didn't want to grow up to be like either one of them.

I was fed well. I had a nice room, a computer, and a bunch of expensive video games that I quickly grew bored with. My parents would buy me only the so-called best of brand name clothing. For such a weird kid I was always well-dressed. But I knew there was more to be had from life. Someday I hoped to work on a SETI project as a scientist or possibly train chimpanzees to speak with sign language. My preference for employment would be working with either aliens or chimps, but not people. My communication skills with my own species were remarkably weak.

My mother would say, "Simon, you can do whatever you want with your life as long as you have a solid education and apply yourself to something practical."

Practical was not any area that was on my radar.

"Simon," my father would say, "you can become whatever you would like to be. Just strive to be the best." These were the words coming from a man who had descended from an alpha male ape. Being the best at something sounded exhausting.

The house resonated with my parents' arguments over money or me. It seeped into the walls and ceilings and floors. The living room carpet soaked up lectures about success that meant little to me. The furniture absorbed my mother's late-night strategies for selling an expensive house to a man of modest means. The paintings on the walls changed colours sometimes if both parents were in the room together arguing about whose money was really carrying the household.

I did not like all the woe that piled up around the house like the old newspapers and magazines I kept in my room for my clipping file. I tried changing my parents into people I would have liked better but failed. They were pretty powerful hominids. I did not hate my parents. I felt sorry for them, but they refused my pity.

I did succeed in creating a force field around my room that kept all their negativity outside my private domain. This was achieved after taking advice from Lydia, the downtown psychic. She was this crazy ex-hippie who read tarot cards and palms or told you about your previous lives. I met her first at the psychic fair on Downey Street. She charged me ten dollars to tell me about my past life as a soldier in Napoleon's army. She said she too had been a soldier in Napoleon's army and I had saved her life in the battle at Waterloo. She insisted we become friends, although "allies" was the word I think she used. Lydia also looked at my hands very closely and announced to anyone within earshot at the psychic fair, "These are the hands of a healer." She held up my hands for everyone to take note. Once that was established, she didn't charge me anymore for advice or psychic services. Teaching me to create an anti-negativity force field she said was "on the house."

Inside, seated at the kitchen table, it seemed that there were voices talking to me, all saying the same thing. The refrigerator telling me Andrea could not possibly exist, the microwave telling me to get a grip on my life. The goddamn toaster suggesting a reality check. I turned on the radio to distract the voices and that didn't help. So I went upstairs and turned on my computer, let the dog outside where it peed on the lawn and barked at the sound of imaginary cars programmed into the software.

CHAPTER SIX

I would not tell my parents about Andrea, but I needed to tell someone. So I told Lydia.

Her apartment was tiny, a cramped living space above a used record store down on Argyle Street. She had no doorbell, no buzzer. An old used envelope tacked to the door said simply, "Go upstairs and walk in. You are expected." Her idea of a psychic's joke.

Old tabloid newspapers were piled on the steps up to her place, some with headlines like, "Elvis found Alive and Well Living Among Baboons." Or "Hitler's Son a Proctologist in Miami."

I knocked on the door and walked in. The smell in the air was a combination of garlic and marijuana. Lydia called the marijuana an "herb," and she seemed quite open about the fact that she was a toker. Never once did she offer me any or even ask if I had ever smoked. I was now a nontoker and a non-drinker. I didn't want to mess with what-ever natural chemical process was going on in my brain. That's why I snubbed even the store-bought pharmaceu-ticals my parents were squandering their money on.

"Hey there," Lydia said as a smoke alarm went off in the tiny kitchen where she was burning something in a frying pan. I walked in and tried to reach for the alarm, but I wasn't tall enough. The shrill sound hurt my ears. Lydia cursed loudly at it and failed to make it stop so she swatted it with a broom, knocking it onto the floor where it split open and spilled its battery, then fell silent.

"Simon, I knew you'd be over today. It's about a girl, isn't it?"

I smiled and sat down on a piece of plastic lawn fur-niture that served as a kitchen chair.

"Good guess," I said.

"I never guess," she said. "I know."

Everyone around town thought Lydia was a phony. Few believed in her psychic powers. I'm not sure I did either. But Lydia was my friend. After Ozzie left town, she became the only person I could talk to about every-thing and anything. She was opinionated but kind. And I needed that.

"A skeleton goes into a bar and asks for a drink," she says. "And the bartender tells him ..."

"I've heard it before," I said.

"Just testing your memory."

"My memory is fine. How are you?"

Lydia had henna purple hair. She wore a long, free-flowing kind of gown or dress that reached the floor. She had funny eyebrows, having plucked her real hairs out and inscribed two straight lines with an indelible marker high above her eyes. Her eyes themselves were unusual. One was green and one brown. She was maybe thirty, possibly older. I never asked.

She scraped whatever she had been cooking into the trash can and apologized for the smell and the smoke. "Let's go into my office," she said, leading me into the little living room where the walls were covered, every inch, with astrological charts.

She flopped down into an old beanbag chair and offered me the famous wicker seat — famous because she claimed the wicker chair held traces of the personality of every person who had ever sat in it. "And there have been some amazing characters that have shown up here over the years," she said.

"About the girl," I began.

"Is she pretty?"

"Yes."

"What's her sign?"

"I don't know."

"My guess would be she's a Capricorn. That's because the moon is in your first house so that makes you shy and moody and it would be attractive to a

Capricorn right about now. Tell me a bit about her. Is it her body that attracts you to her or her heart?"

"Well, it can't be her body because I don't think she is real. I mean in the corporeal sense."

"I see. What makes you think she's not corporeal?"

"No one else but me can see her."

"But she looks like a regular girl?"

"Define regular."

"Hmm. What about her clothes? She had clothes, didn't she?"

"Her clothes seemed like something a girl at my school would wear. Nothing special."

"So she's probably contemporary, not someone from the past."

"Seemed like she was here and now."

"I still think she must be a Capricorn. Are you in love with her?"

"I don't think so. In fact, I think I finally got Tanya Webb to notice me. Or I think my new friend did something to make Tanya like me."

"Wow. Some friend. This Tanya, is she real?"

"She is, and she has a great corporeal presence."

"Be careful. Tanya sounds like trouble."

Lydia lit some incense even though she knew I didn't like the smell of patchouli. She walked to the window and blew some dust off a large dream catcher, making it swing freely in the sunlight.

"The other one have a name?"

"Andrea."

"Does she frighten you?"

"Not at all."

"Do you sense *anything* about her that is foreboding?"

"No. She just looks confused sometimes like she's trying to figure something out."

"Why do you think she appeared to you?"

"She says she's here to help me."

"What do you think?"

"Maybe she is."

Lydia seemed at a loss for words. "You know I'm between spirit guides right now. Kassan said he had to move on, and I'm waiting to make contact with a new guide. So far, no go. Oh, I can contact plenty of spirits, but there are so many that are unreliable. What a bunch of jokers." She changed the subject. "You shouldn't slouch so much. You want to keep your spine straight so you can absorb as much energy from the sun as you can and direct it to all your vital organs."

Lydia probably had a form of ADD too. She jumped around a lot, called herself a "non-linear thinker." "How's your chess game?" she asked.

"I won three in a row against a hotshot on the Internet. I'm getting better."

She nodded her approval, switched back to the main subject. "A contemporary girl appears out of thin air to a young man in school," she said, stroking her cheek with two fingers. "I think you should build this relationship with caution."

"I wasn't thinking about marrying her."

"That's comforting. But I would still be careful. Don't do anything to upset her. She could be the one in a vulnerable state."

"She seems to have things under control. Maybe all I have to do is sit back and let her help me."

"The energy has to flow in two directions."

"Have you had this sort of thing happen to you?"

"My guides are always very real to me but not in any physical sense. I can see a face maybe while I am in a trance, but no, they don't sit down on the furniture and watch *Oprah* with me or anything like that."

"Then this girl is unusual."

"Unusual but not impossible. I think you have been selected somehow."

"Chosen?"

"Either verb will do."

"I guess I was kinda hoping you could look into the future and tell me what might happen next. I really don't want to screw this up."

Lydia laughed. "Do you see a crystal ball anywhere around here? I know I've given you warnings and advice in the past but I haven't ever *predicted* what will happen. I don't like to mess with free will."

"Maybe just give me a heads-up."

She breathed in deeply. "There's not one of the spirits I'm in communication with that I can currently trust. They are all rascals. I'm not even giving them the time of day. You want advice? Be nice to her. Don't push things. Trust your instincts."

"Sheesh," I said. "Very profound."

Lydia laughed. Those funny eyebrows were two high thin lines rising up on her forehead.

"I've been afraid to ask her this, but I'd really like to know exactly *what* she is."

"If I were you, I'd worry less about *what* she is and stay focused on *who* she is. Labels always have a way of screwing things up. You should know that better than anyone."

Lydia began to rearrange some small crystal rocks in a bowl she had on the coffee table. I thanked her for her time and said I'd stay in touch.

"I'm positive she's a Capricorn," Lydia asserted as I walked out the door.

Dinner was Chinese takeout, which I hated. My parents both used chopsticks to eat their food. They thought themselves very clever. I opted for a microwaved pizza with special cardboard flavouring (the NEW AND IMPROVED aspect, I supposed) and two fortune cookies. One said, "You are about to experience the respect you deserve," and the other said, "A modest man never talks of himself." An interesting combination.

My mother was going on and on about a house she had just "listed." My father was wondering out loud if it was going to rain on the weekend and spoil his golf game. I asked if I could have some money to go bungee jumping at the new place called Over the Edge.

"No way," my dad said, punctuating the denial by tapping his chopsticks together in front of him.

"Simon, be realistic," my mother said. "No way / be realistic" was a kind of household chant, an all-purpose dual parent response to any of my serious questions. I didn't tell them about Andrea, naturally, and I wouldn't bother getting the dirty looks by telling them I went to visit Lydia.

The argument between my mom and dad started over something small — some flaw in the phoned-in order involving sweet and sour sauce. Then it escalated into World War Three. Fortunately for all of us, my parents were only verbal types and didn't get physical. They said unkind things to each other, pointing out this shortcoming and that flaw and then they almost always brought me, or at least the subject of me, into the battlefield.

"If you'd been a better mother — if you'd instilled some common sense into your son — he may have been ..."

"Normal" is the word my father did not say. He paused right there in the heat of battle, as if realizing for the first time that I was still in the room.

"You bastard," my mother said, stealing a look at me as if she were coming to my defence. "How dare you!" She had both volume and resonance in her voice. My father looked like he had just stepped in a cow pie. He threw down his chopsticks and left the room.

For many years after my skateboard accident (which I refer to as my "lobotomy," although the term is not really accurate) I wondered if my parents would have been better off without me in their lives. I often believed myself to be the cause of their unhappiness. Lying in bed at night, I wondered if there was some better place for me to be — better for them, better for me. So, thanks to some serious book study, I would astrally project myself, leaving my body and travelling up this long silvery thread into the night sky and off to anywhere I wanted to go.

Sometimes that took me to a beach in Australia where it was daytime and there were lots of well-tanned girls and many friendly and wise young men surfers who liked me. They said things like "Fair dinkum" to anything I said. I wanted to surf badly and asked to borrow a board. "Sure, mate," one bushy-headed blonde guy said. "Go get tubed."

But every time my big toe touched the sea, I was yanked back into my body on the other side of the planet.

I woke up early the next day and walked to school, down the old railway track hiking trail. I expected Andrea to appear, but she did not. At school, however, I saw her at the far end of the hall and she waved, but as I approached she walked away. I found my locker and fumbled with my books. Some days my mind is clear about school — where to go when, which books to take. Today was not one of those days. I looked at my schedule taped to my locker door; I selected the books I needed. And then I looked up and realized Tanya Webb was standing there. She was smiling.

"I have a report to write about Druids for Hist. Civ. class and I don't know where to begin. I was wondering if you might help."

The fortune cookie was right.

"I'd love to. The Druids built Stonehenge, you know?" This was my version of flirtation. I realize it was not typical of Stockton High, but a door had opened here into another dimension — the dimension of encounters with the opposite sex.

"That's in England isn't it?"

"Sure. The Druids were Celts."

"Were they short?"

"Not necessarily. You shouldn't mix up Druids and dwarfs."

Tanya just smiled, and I pinched myself to see if I was really in school or still home in bed, imagining all this.

Then I saw Andrea standing behind Tanya. Andrea waved but slid her fingers across her mouth like it was a zipper, reminding me not to say anything out loud to her. Andrea had tweaked something in Tanya's mind to make her feel kindly towards me.

"Let's meet in the public library after school, okay?" I boldly said. The bell was about to ring.

"Sure. See you then," Tanya said and walked on. I just stood there and watched her walk. She did it extremely nicely.

"That went well," Andrea said.

"Did you do that?"

"I knew she had a paper on Druids and figured here was a window."

"A window?"

"An opportunity. Remember, I'm here to help you."

"You're here to help me with girls?"

"I'm here to help you in general. You are a loner, Simon. You spend too much time by yourself, too much time inside your head."

"It's true. Anyway, I appreciate it. Are you coming with me to class?"

"Which one?"

I had forgotten already. Rats. I had to look at my schedule again and realized that it was Thursday. "Math. And I didn't do the homework."

"Let's go."

Mr. Michaels nailed me not five minutes into the class. "Simon, do problem 3 on page 147. At the board."

Many other teachers took pity on me and didn't send me to the board. Not Michaels. Humiliation was his forte.

I got out of my seat and carried my book to the front of the class. Andrea was right behind me. I wrote the long equation on the chalkboard and didn't have a clue as to where to begin to find out what X equalled. I took a deep breath and began to turn to look at Mr. Michaels and give him my long-practised and well-rehearsed shrug when Andrea took my arm and began to move my hand.

I giggled. The class laughed. Michaels scowled.

"Get serious," a voice said.

I cleared my throat and pretended to be studying the equation. I moved letters and numbers from one side of the equation to the other. I crossed some things out. There appeared to be multiplication and division involved. I seemed to know what to do with the parenthesis. And then, suddenly, I had discovered that X equalled Y minus 19.

My hand set the chalk down. Andrea let go, but I could still feel a kind of energy radiating in my hand from where she had held it. I turned around. Michaels looked puzzled. "That is correct," he said flatly, "although I wouldn't have done those steps quite in that order."

I sat back down in my seat and Mr. Michaels picked the next victim — Parker, who was looking a little pale.

Andrea stood by the window through the rest of math but vanished again when I wasn't looking at her. I didn't see her again until lunch. Tanya waved at me from a table where she was sitting with her friends. I waved back but decided I would blunder if I tried to sit with her and those other girls. Instead, I sat alone with my tray of meat loaf and macaroni, my can of Dr. Pepper, and my thoughts. And then someone touched my elbow. I turned and there she was.

I told her about Lydia, and she didn't seem too pleased. "You asked her about me?"

"I have a hard enough time figuring out basic stuff. You are something quite unusual. Unique. I needed some thoughts from someone I trust."

Andrea seemed a little hurt. "You don't trust me?"

"What's there not to trust? You make a girl like me. You save my ass at the board in math. I've known Lydia for a long time. She's my friend."

"Maybe she's the one that you shouldn't trust. I don't believe in psychics or people who claim to talk to spirits," Andrea said.

That was a twist. I decided not to ask her why an appearing and vanishing girl did not believe in psychics or mediums. "Okay. But she's a good friend. As you've noticed, I don't have many."

"You want to be voted most popular for the yearbook?"

"No thanks."

"Okay. Just be careful what you say about me and to whom. I'm in a kind of vulnerable position and I'm still new at this."

That's when I realized that some of the kids noticed I was talking out loud to no one. I had only been whispering and I had been covering my mouth so I didn't look so obvious, but I guess it was still pretty apparent.

I looked into Andrea's eyes and repeated her gesture — finger across the mouth. Keep it zipped.

Then I looked around the room. A few people were staring. I smiled at them like everything was normal. I would have to keep my wits about me. I would have to be more careful.

In the split second when I had looked away from her, Andrea was gone. She had either gotten up and run off or she had vanished into thin air, and I was left alone with my cold meat loaf and a new sense of confusion, enough to send me back to my locker to check my schedule to figure out where I had to go next. I realized

I might have to make it through the rest of the day on my own.

CHAPTER SEVEN

For the rest of the school day I was on my own. And I did wonder often where Andrea went. Was it a matter of geography, of time, of different planes of existence? Or was she still *there*? Could she simply control who could see her and when?

I should have been nervous about my after-school meeting with Tanya but I wasn't. I was in fortune cookie mode. I had good planets in the right houses. I had Andrea influencing Tanya's interest in me. I figured I was pretty much just along for the ride. And it was about time.

My interest in girls had always been there, but it seemed like a lost cause. I was a kid with many labels — some polite, some not. Oddly enough I was rarely a victim. Guys didn't pick on me because of the way I am. If someone made fun of me for saying something stupid in class, I laughed along with everyone else. I learned a long time ago that the best self-defence is sometimes no defence at all. Laugh at yourself when they are laughing at you and you defuse their power.

Andrea, on my behalf, had changed Tanya's view of me from peculiar to interesting. If you think about it, the two aren't that far apart. I wanted to thank Andrea, but she wasn't anywhere to be seen at school at the end of the day, so I walked down the street to the library and there was Tanya sitting at a table alone. I saw her through the window and my heart leaped in my chest. "Just try to avoid acting like an idiot," I counselled myself. At least I assume it was me giving advice to myself in my head. "Be cool," the voice said. "Like ice," I replied.

Tanya was doodling in her notebook.

"Hi," I said.

"Thanks for coming," she said.

I sat down. "So you're interested in Druids?"

She nodded. "Well, I'm curious. They seem so mysterious. But I don't know where to begin ... my research, I mean."

"We could get a few books."

Tanya seemed to think that using the computer to look up the call numbers of books and then actually finding the books was brilliant on my part. It wasn't like rocket science, but maybe she was just trying to be nice to me.

"I really appreciate you helping me."

"Sure. No problem. In fact, first let me tell you what I already know about Druids."

My head was stuffed with an encyclopaedia of information regarding the occult, mysticism, the para-normal. What I had read stayed with me — almost all of it. But I couldn't retrieve it easily. I suppose it had something to do with the brain damage. In order to remember things, I would have to use memory tricks. For example, if I closed my eyes and pretended I was in the desert, and then started looking for something by digging in the sand, I would find what I was looking for. Or I could imagine I was on a lake and go fishing for an answer with a fishing pole. And find it.

Tanya studied my face as I closed my eyes. I went to a rocky coastline this time. It looked like Cornwall in England, and I was looking for a stone that had the dope on Druids. It was just beneath a high cliff with a cascading waterfall.

"The Druids were like religious leaders, healers some of them. I think they cured sick people with herbs and plants. They worshipped the sun and they believed in the immortality of the soul."

I could open my eyes now and remember more once I had started to tap into the information in my memory. Tanya was taking notes. She had the most beautiful handwriting I'd ever seen — like flowers in a garden. "What do you think about the immortality of the soul?" I asked her, thinking this was a clever segue into getting to know her better.

She stopped writing. "I don't know what you mean."

I realized I was not very good at small talk with girls. "I was just wondering if you thought we lived on after we died or what."

"Wow," she said. "That's a big question. I guess something must happen. What do you think?"

I swallowed. I should probably not go there. I had seven different theories, all quite plausible, about what happens when you die, but if I were to tell Tanya, I figured it would be the end of our "friendship." So I just said, "I think the soul lives on."

"Cool," she said, pleased with the brevity of my answer.

"So the Druids lived in France and southern England. They built monuments to the sun — like Stonehenge, for example, where they set up a circle of very large stones."

"But I thought they were quite short."

"Not necessarily, although I think everybody was shorter in those days. And they didn't live as long as we do."

"That's too bad. But do you think they had any fun?"

Hmm. I didn't know if the Druids had any fun. They seemed kind of serious from what I read, but I hoped they had fun so I made something up. "They had lots of parties and drank a concoction made from fermented honey. And they had great music."

How could the Druids *not* have had great music? Tanya was back to taking notes, but I'd been distracted from my memory search. I closed my eyes again and saw some Druids dancing on a cliff above the waterfalls. Oh boy.

"The Druids were the religious leaders of people called the Celts — that's with a C — and they held worship ceremonies in sacred groves. They had fires and burned things as sacrifices. They worshipped the sun, but they believed the earth too had sacred powers and some Druids could feel the energy along certain paths. Some Druids could use willow branches to find water deep under the earth."

"How do you know all this stuff?"

"I read a lot of books."

"I read mostly magazines. But this is really great stuff." She looked at me so sweetly I thought I would melt, but she seemed almost sleepy and I think she was stifling a yawn.

I didn't know what else to do but ramble on some more about Stonehenge and the sun worship, and when all I had left was stuff about fertility rituals I told her, "Fertility of the earth and people were intermingled in the Druids' religion. Some plants were considered to have powers to make women more fertile — you know, so they could have sex and have more babies."

Tanya was dutifully taking notes. "Mistletoe, for example — the berries were said to represent human male sperm. It was considered a sacred plant to the Druids. In fact, the custom of kissing beneath mistletoe at Christmas is like a leftover from some Druid ritual involving mistletoe." But that was as far as I was willing to explain anything about fertility rites.

I waited for Tanya to look up, wondering if she was going to think I was getting too creepy. Instead, she just said, "That's really fascinating. I never knew that about mistletoe."

"It's a little-known fact."

I dredged up some other details about stone circles and more on the Druids' ideas of immortality and Tanya seemed to be genuinely impressed.

A car was blowing its horn outside on the street: two long, one short. "That's for me," Tanya said. "It's my mom. She never gets out of the car when she picks me up anywhere. Just two long and one short. You've been great." Then she touched my hand and as she stood up and she smiled at me again. "Let's get together again," she said. "I want to pick your brain some more about ancient rituals."

As she was about to leave the library, she turned and blew me a kiss.

At that point I had forgotten all about Andrea. I had never had a girl like Tanya give me so much attention and I was in a kind of swoon — foggy in the head, getting up and floating down the aisles through the bookshelves. I turned a corner and nearly ran right into Andrea standing there leafing through a book about vampires.

"And how did that go?"

"Fine," I answered. "I really like her. She has an inquiring mind."

"And a nice set of boobs," Andrea said sarcastically.

I think I blushed. "She was nice to me because of you, right?"

"Correct," Andrea said, a cool breeze in her voice.

"And I don't really stand a chance?"

Andrea didn't say anything. She smirked. At least that's what I think that look was on her face.

Andrea looked down at her book and turned the page, pretending to read it. After I stood silently for a few minutes, she looked up. "What are you waiting for?" she asked.

I wasn't sure what to say. I felt flustered. Puzzled. "I don't know. I guess I figured that if you were here, you were here to talk to me about something."

She seemed downright angry now, closed her book, and said, "You think it's always about you, don't you?" She slid the book back onto the shelf and then went down the next aisle into the fiction section. I followed, but as expected, when I looked down the next aisle she was gone.

CHAPTER EIGHT

Once when I was fifteen, I was walking to the mall on a winter day near sunset when I looked out into a field and saw a tree that seemed to be on fire. But there was no smoke, just the fire of the sun shining through the leafless branches. I felt paralyzed, but in a good way. It was the kind of feeling I expected if ever aliens transported me up into a spacecraft.

Immobility and a kind of diffuse feeling of well-being. I felt myself being drawn toward the light even though I was not moving. I felt like I was one with the tree and one with the sun. And no, I had not been toking up (marijuana makes me cough) and I was not taking anything illegal or over-the-counter.

I think this feeling, this sense of overwhelming connection and awe, lasted for nearly a minute. Then the sun was dropping beneath the horizon and it was gone.

I felt cold and alone and infinitely sad, for what I had experienced was so brief.

I kept expecting the same thing to happen again. But it didn't. I tried to *make* it happen but it wasn't there. It was like a fleeting window had opened up to another world, another way of being, another me — and then that window was gone, maybe forever.

Lydia was the only one I could talk to about this. I did not mention it to my parents or there would have been more money wasted on prescriptions I would not take. Lydia made me feel like I wasn't crazy.

"The Japanese Zen Buddhists call it a *satori*. Wham. It just hits you, usually triggered by something. Something beautiful but not always. You could be walking down the street on a dull, dreary afternoon and it could happen."

"What does it mean?"

"It means everything is connected to everything else, if you'll pardon my New Age vernacular. If we are lucky, every once in a while we just feel this to be true. You had your *satori*. You were a lucky boy. I felt the same thing once sitting in an airplane of all places. Coming home from a psychic fair in Ottawa. There was a rainbow at the end of the runway, and when we took off through the arch of the rainbow it followed us up into the clouds and changed into a perfect circle around the plane. We flew through the centre of it and then it vanished. Nobody else on the plane seemed to notice or care. Except for me."

"So it doesn't mean I'm crazy?"

Lydia laughed and then straightened a pile of palmistry books sitting on the table. "Oh, you're freaking crazy all right. You'd rather be normal?"

"I don't know what normal is."

"Don't go there. You wouldn't like it."

I waited impatiently for the next *satori*. Music almost took me there once. It was close but not the real thing. I went back to the tree at sunset again. It was pretty, but no cigar. I went there at sunrise once but it wouldn't give.

As usual, I turned to books for some more insight into this and discovered that the ancient Chinese were a bit more interested in the *satori* experience than us busy modern folk in designer shirts and pants. It was common for someone in ancient China to have the *satori* experience and want to achieve it again. While reading about ancient waterfalls and the sound of tiny ancient birds, I recalled my own vision of the beach and the surfer pouring skateboard ball bearings into my hands. I saw there was a connection between the way I had felt then in that "other" world and the tree. Just like my experience with the tree *satori*, I had tried to get back there to that beach — in my mind, at least.

I could imagine the place, but I could never feel that feeling of being there.

One ancient Chinese dude named Wu-men explained that *satori* comes only after you have exhausted your thinking, only when "the mind can no longer grasp itself."

At school my English teacher, Mr. Pace, got mad at me for reading about Zen while he was lecturing us on pronouns. I had been bored out of my gourd as he droned on about subjective, possessive, and objective pronouns. So I picked up my Zen book and began to read. Many of my classmates had perfected the semi-conscious hibernetic mode of pronoun lecture survival where they looked like they were paying attention but they were a million miles away. Maybe this mode of mental and physical separation was something practised by ancient Chinese masters as well, I don't know.

As far as Mr. Pace was concerned, he was drilling those pronoun rules into our thick skulls, turning us into better speakers, immaculate writers who knew where and when to use the right words. To Mr. Pace, grammar was probably a kind of religion. Maybe he found his own *satori* among the right combination of nouns and verbs, adverbs and adjectives.

But he was fully and perfectly insulted when he looked my way and saw that I was not pretending to pay attention. I was reading a book on Zen, which was at that moment suggesting to me that "to travel is better than to arrive" and that "man is a process not an entity." These ideas were real corkers and demanded all my attention.

"Simon," Mr. Pace said in a rather nasal and negative voice. "Simon, what do you think you are doing?"

Well, this drew everyone in the class back to a third period plane of existence. Heads turned. I was sitting there with my book open, a bit blatant I suppose. I felt my cheeks getting red. Had I been looking at a *Playboy* magazine, things would not have been so bad. Had it been a pornographic comic or a magazine about growing weed or even a motorcycle magazine, it would not have been such a problem.

"I guess I got distracted," I said, closing my book, blinking at the words on the board: *Objective, subjective, possessive*.

Mr. Pace liked the fact that he now had the attention of the class and that he had a victim. Well, maybe he wasn't sadistic; he just had an opportunity to flaunt his authority and get away with a little humiliation, which is a kind of fringe benefit for some teachers. "Exactly what are you reading about that's so much more important than grammar?"

"Enlightenment, sir," I said. I threw in "sir" because I thought it would get me off the hook, and it was the term that all the ancient Chinese students of Tao used when referring to their own masters who would ask them questions like "What is the sound of one hand clapping?"

The class roared in laughter. I was the perfect fool, in their minds. Only Simon would sit in English class and do something as goofy as read about religion, wasting good daydreaming time, existing in his own weird little planet, his own dimension. And Mr. Pace laughed along with them.

I had said nothing more. I took my humiliation, swallowed hard, saw the look on Davis Conroy's face, the look on all their faces. I saw a small spider working on a web up in the front corner of the room near the flag. I watched it and allowed my mind to distance itself from my body.

To say that Tanya Webb and I had a relationship is probably stretching it. She received a B+ for her Druid report and considered herself, under my tutelage, to be something of a world expert on the subject. My reward was an actual hug and a peck on the cheek. I helped with her homework in the library a couple more times. I was always more interested in her homework than mine. I maintained my usual plan of trying to get through high school on autopilot, expending only minimal brain activity on the curriculum and preferring all the extracurricular possibilities of learning. I was one of those students proud to achieve a C and felt lucky to nail down a C+ sometimes as a pity grade from a teacher who knew I was smart but "had problems."

With Tanya showing some interest in me — she always remained friendly with me even when the homework was over — other girls would at least talk to me now. They asked my opinion about the latest reality-based TV shows. I almost never watched TV except for old *Star Trek* reruns or rented DVDs like *The Matrix* or *Blade Runner*.

My opinion on the latest TV crap thrust on the mindless proletariat? "It's hard to pick a favourite," I would say. And then I would smile a kind of warm, vacant smile and I would give good eye contact. That was Andrea's idea. "Give them eye contact. Hold it until they turn away first."

Phew. Simple little manoeuvre. But it worked. I didn't stare. I didn't ogle the way the other members of my male half of the population like to do. I didn't try to overpower them with my penetrating gaze. I just gave good eye contact. It took some practice in front of the mirror to get it right.

"And say their names," Andrea further advised. *See you later, Jennifer. Hi, Candace. Yo, Venetia.*

"Say nice things about their clothes or hair," she continued.

"I can't do that," I said. "It doesn't feel like me."

Well, I did try it on Tanya when I thought Andrea wasn't around, although I never really knew for sure when she was around. Tanya liked the compliments. Oddly enough, she seemed to be happiest when I told her that I liked her shoes. "Great shoes," I said.

"You like them?" she said enthusiastically.

"I love them."

The shoes looked like average girl footwear. I was slipping over to the dark side.

After homework one day in the library, I walked Tanya home — one small step for mankind. Before I said goodbye, I gave her the full range of compliments. After I left Tanya and began walking home, there was Andrea.

"It's really important to her, you know?"

"What is?"

"Footwear." She wasn't smiling.

It was two weeks into the new improved me. "You taught me everything I know. It's really quite amazing. I've graduated from class dweeb to social respectability. I guess this is how you were supposed to help me."

"Maybe it is."

I suddenly remembered my discussion with Lydia. "What's your sign anyway?"

"My what?"

"Your astrological sign."

"Capricorn. Why?"

"Just curious, I guess." Lydia had been right.

Then, as I looked at her, I realized something was wrong. While I had been changing, Andrea had been changing, too. At first she had been fun to be around. Now she was serious. And elusive. She appeared less often. Did I detect that she seemed to have less ... colour? A kind of pallor.

"I really like your hair," I said.

"Idiot." But she liked the compliment.

I was giving eye contact. Andrea had often deflected my questions about her, and I had assumed that I should quit asking. But we'd known each other a long time — two weeks seemed like a long time — and she knew everything about me, even the embarrassing stuff, and I knew nothing about her. "Do you have, um, parents?" I asked.

Something changed drastically in her eyes. I felt that weird sensation of her moving away from me even though her feet were not going anywhere. "Okay, forget it. I won't ask. But someday I hope you'll tell me about you. Who you are. Where you're from."

She took a step closer. "I'm worried that I might be losing you," she blurted out.

"Losing me. How?" I asked.

But I heard a car stop just then behind me. I turned and saw it was a police car. Andrea was gone.

A boy standing on the sidewalk having an intent conversation with a hedge sometimes prompts a lawman to make an inquiry.

"I'm in a school play. I was just practising," I explained.

He was a young officer with one of these lawn-mower haircuts. He had a kind of pudginess to the sides of his head, a soft layer of fat that was all too obvious thanks to the close-cropped hair. I was thinking I'd seen cops like him before, that maybe he was a clone. But I didn't ask.

"You live around here?"

"I'm just walking home. From school. It's a long walk, but I like the exercise."

He was still sizing me up. Drug freak? Stone head? Potential terrorist?

"You want a ride home?" he asked, testing me.

"Sure," I answered, thinking this was probably better than making him more suspicious.

"Hop in."

It was not exactly as expected. I was sitting in the back like a criminal with the wire mesh between the front seat and the back. The radio was squawking. There was a rifle attached to the dashboard. I wasn't usually a paranoid guy, but this was making me nervous. From this angle, buddy with the Lawnboy hair and the puffy fat sides looked rather like an alien. I wondered if they were finally abducting me.

"You follow baseball?" he asked.

"Sometimes," I said, knowing that some men didn't

trust kids who had no interest in sports. I was one of those kids.

"I'm a Red Sox fan," he said, offering me a piece of gum through the wire mesh. I took the gum, having passed some kind of test.

"Yankees," I said. "I'm a huge Yankees fan."

"I always hated the Yankees."

"They're that kind of team. You either love 'em or you hate 'em."

He laughed and shook his head. I had cracked the code. I was okay. I'd either get dropped off at my house or the cop car would make a vertical liftoff and we'd go directly to the mother ship.

He stopped in front of my house. "Sit tight, kid. I have to open the door from the outside."

I got out. "Thanks for the ride," I said.

"Forget the Yankees. They've had their day. It's over."

"Yeah, maybe. I don't know."

"Good luck with the play. What's it called? Maybe I'll come see it."

Crap. I couldn't think for a second, tried hard to remember what the school play was. "*Macbeth*," I said.

"Right."

Both cars were in the driveway. And it was only four-thirty. Not a good sign. I felt a small pool of dread growing in my chest. Had the game of golf been outlawed? Had the real estate market gone flat? I looked around the yard to see if Andrea might have followed me, but the yard was empty. The grass had been clipped immaculately by the landscaping people. Flowers bloomed with great intent. A newspaper was rolled up and sitting on the walkway.

CHAPTER NINE

My mother and my father were sitting at the kitchen table. My plan was to say hi and retreat to my room. Whatever was going on, I didn't want to be part of it. They looked very sullen.

"Simon, we need to talk to you," my mother said, her voice sounding shaky.

"Sit down with us, would you?" my father added, trying to sound like he was in control.

If ever there was a good time to escape from reality, this was it. But I didn't have any easy way out.

I sat down reluctantly. I guessed that they had finally figured out I wasn't taking my medication.

"Simon, you know your mother and I don't always get along," my dad began.

"We have very different personalities," my mom said. "We've tried to work things out over the years ..."

"For your sake," Dad said, bringing me into the equation. "But we feel that we've hit a point where staying together is not a good thing for any of us."

"It's called a trial separation," my mom stated flatly and then looked around the room as if she was searching for something, but it was just a matter of avoiding looking at me. I looked away from her as well and was shocked to see Andrea standing by the refrigerator. My mother seemed to be looking right at her. Andrea indicated I should not react. Why was she here? Why now?

My father loosened his tie. "I'm moving out, but your mother is staying here. Maybe you and I can go to the beach this weekend." He had never offered this before. "Maybe we can spend some quality time together."

"We're sorry to have to put you through all this. You must have been able to see it was coming."

I felt numb. I couldn't wrestle any words out of my mouth. I looked over at Andrea — who appeared so frightened. I peered into her eyes, deep into them, and it scared me.

"Simon, why are you staring like that? Talk to me please," my mom said.

"What do you want me to say?"

"Tell me what you feel."

I sat quietly, looked away from all of them, and stared down at the newspaper sitting on the table in front of me. The words seemed to be rearranging themselves on the page. I was angry and frightened. Both. Angry at them for doing this to me. They weren't like the best parents in the world but they were my parents and they'd always been around. They had always tried to do what they thought was best for me. I was not number one on their list of priorities but at least I had been on the list somewhere. They had done their duty. And I knew they had always cared as much as they were capable of caring. But now this.

As if to shift the blame away from them, my father changed the subject, the bastard. "We've had a couple of calls from school — about your behaviour. Incidents of talking to yourself."

This wasn't fair. My old man was about to bail out on his family, bail out on me, and now he was going to talk to me about acting weird in school.

"I know this is not the best time to bring it up — we haven't sat down to talk together for a while. But have you been taking your medication?"

Oh, so it did come out after all. Andrea was pacing back and forth. I think she was having a hard time being here in this house, in the midst of this kind of situation.

"I've been doing just fine. I take my pills," I lied.

"We just needed to know for sure," my dad said. "We are concerned about your well-being." Very formal. Very professional.

I took a deep breath. A strange bit of calm came over me then as if I could channel the anger and the hurt I was feeling and keep it contained in one part of my brain. *I will get through this*, I told myself. Watching Andrea pace back and forth making nervous gestures with her hands, it suddenly occurred to me that this was all somehow worse for her than for me. She would approach the back door and then turn around and come back towards us. She held out her hand as if to turn the door handle but then reversed herself and came towards me with that look of fear in her eyes. This whole scene was doing something awful to her.

I got up and walked to the door, opened it. Andrea came towards me, paused, then put her head down and walked outside. "I'm so sorry," she said, barely audible. And then she ran.

"Simon?"

"It's okay, Mom. I just needed some air." Looking out at our front yard — the flowers, the green leaves of the trees — I had this funny realization of how much I loved that front yard. Even the grass. I loved the grass. But it was more than that. I loved this, my home. Despite all the arguing, despite the usual parental hassles. Despite everything, this was my home. And now all that was going to change forever. My parents would separate. I would see my father rarely. He was always terrible at keeping father-to-son promises. He would get even worse at it, I was sure.

And my mother. She had often talked about moving to a condo. How long before she would want to sell the house — this one where I grew up?

"I'm going to my room now," I told them.

"We're sorry about all this," my mom said.

My dad put his hands up like he was trying to shape something in the air in front of him. He wanted to say something that would make me feel better, but he knew the English language had no words that could help him here. "I'm going to pack some of my things," my father said. "Maybe you and I can go out for pizza, Simon, before I take off."

"Sure, Dad," I said.

In my room, I took my big pair of sharp, pointed scissors out of my desk and I jabbed the points once into the wooden desktop. Then I sat down on the floor and began going through the pile of newspapers there. Ever since I was little I had been working on what I called my research — clipping and filing articles on space travel, UFOs, weird and unusual stuff happening anywhere on the planet. It was a big pile of papers. I guess recently I'd been losing interest in my little hobby. There had been a couple of UFO sightings up north. Crop circles were back in the news. A new research team was looking for the Loch Ness monster. A story about unusual brain activity in a coma patient. A stain on a wall at a McDonald's that appeared to be an image of Jesus Christ. And a report by one seemingly reputable astronomer who had discovered a comet on a dead-centre collision course with earth. Impact would take place in ten thousand years, and he said it was a certainty that all life on earth would be destroyed. Now there was something to get my mind off my own worries.

I wasn't sure why I was collecting these clippings. I had just been doing it for so long. The UFO file was huge. It seemed completely unfair that so many other people had seen UFOs and aliens and I had not.

There was a knock at my door. "It's open."

My dad walked in looking like he was guilty of a crime. "Simon," he said. "This will turn out all right for you, I promise."

"Do you really have to do this?"

"I do. It's been a long time coming, but your mom and I both know we have to get away from each other. Maybe just for a while."

"Or maybe for good?"

"We don't know."

"You guys argue a lot about me, I know. Maybe I'm the one at fault here."

"It's not like that." My father sat down on the floor, looked at my files of clippings. He opened the one about strange weather phenomena. "Frogs really fall from the sky?"

"Sometimes," I said. "And fish. They get caught in a tornado or maybe a waterspout. They go way up into the clouds and then they have to come down somewhere."

"When I was your age, I wanted to be a scientist. I wanted to split atoms or do undersea research. For a while I thought I would be a science officer on a space mission. Man, I had all kinds of dreams."

"Why didn't you go for it?"

He shrugged. "Well, I did. Sort of. I went to university and took some science courses but wasn't very good at it. I just couldn't hack it. I didn't have what it takes. I got kind of depressed, started drinking, and went further down the tubes. So my father sat me down and said to forget about all this science crap and going to the moon malarky. Get realistic. Get practical. I changed over to business courses and finished university. Then, wham. Just like that I got a job at a bank, then at an investment company. It all just happened. I woke up one morning and had this life. I didn't know if I even liked it, but I was good at it."

"You did okay."

"Nah. I blew it. I didn't see that you were the best thing that happened to me. I let you do most of your growing up on your own."

"You were around."

He kind of snorted. "Around, yeah. But not there. Not here."

"I don't know what happened between you and Mom."

"Your mother changed. She wasn't always like this."

I nodded. I remember a woman who played games with me, one who sang to me when I was little. She was between jobs then. She sang along with songs on the radio and she sat with me to watch Walt Disney videos and we played games with cards. Penny poker. My mother taught me to play penny poker when I was only seven. And she had taught me chess.

"Your mother learned to be the way she is — well, she learned it from me."

It was the first time I think that my father had ever talked to me like this. Like we were equals. I searched for my own words to say something that would help but couldn't find any.

He put his hand on my shoulder. "Gotta go. Let's talk soon, though. I'll call you tomorrow."

I guess he was packing his stuff and my mother sure didn't want to be in the same room with him when that was happening. So it was her turn. She knocked on my door and came in. It was the official Feel Sorry for Simon Day at my house. She brought with her some more newspapers. "Finding anything interesting?" she asked.

"Black holes in space. Talking dogs. Another ten-thousand-year-old man found frozen in a glacier. The usual."

"I wish things could be different."

"I know." I was feeling numbness in my mind and I was fighting it. A great dark thing was settling over me just then and I wanted to scream at my mother and go vent rage at my father. I heard him walking down the stairs and I started to get up, to go say goodbye to him.

"Don't," my mother said. "Just stay here with me. Just let him leave. Please."

I saw Andrea now, by the window. But her back was to me. She was facing the wall and she was shaking. She must have been crying. She was somehow being drawn into my own pain, my own suffering.

I walked over to my desk and opened the drawer. I took out the plastic vial of prescription pills and held them up for my mother to see. "I haven't been taking them. For quite a while."

"We suspected that. Your teachers have been concerned, and sometimes the way you act ..."

"I've heard you both arguing. About me. About what to do with me."

"It's not just you. It's a lot of things."

"If I start taking the meds again, would you try staying together for a while? Give it another chance?"

My mother looked puzzled. A decision had been made. Her mind had already been set. Much arguing and their own suffering had brought them to this day and now I wanted to change all that. I opened the twist-off lid of the vial and popped one of the red pills in my mouth. I grabbed a bottle of water from my desk and swallowed.

I heard the front door open as my father began to walk out of the house. I heard his footsteps on the driveway. When I looked out the window I saw him getting into the car. I looked at my mother. Her head was down. She was crying. "Okay," she said, still crying. "We'll try."

I opened the window and yelled out to my father. "Wait!"

CHAPTER TEN

There was an air of reconciliation around my house. The arguing stopped. I spent less time in my room and the three of us were together more often. It's not that we were doing anything exciting: eating a pizza together, watching a DVD. My father reading the newspaper and handing it to me to look for articles about two-headed chickens and gravity wells. There were still problems between them. That's not something that goes away overnight. It wasn't the thrill of having their boy back on expensive drugs — it wasn't like I was going to be normal or anything. But I had triggered the change and I had to keep up my end of the bargain.

Two pills, three times a day. I was a pharmaceutical wonder. A drug company's answer to corporate profits. The stuff slowed me down some. My thoughts ran more in a straight line. I could stay focused more easily in classes. I could look straight at the teacher instead of darting my eyes around the room. I aced a math quiz, wrote a totally intelligible research essay about the Carthaginians.

My mother took me shopping and I bought some clothes that were in style. I got a haircut.

I missed the old me, I really did. The new me was much less entertaining. But Tanya liked the new me. She said nice things about my clothes and hair. (Is that all that is really necessary to make a girl pay attention? Scary thought.) She had me over to her house for dinner and then her parents went out. We were alone in their living room with their big-screen TV and home theatre surround sound. We were watching her father's collector's edition DVD of one of my all-time favourite films, *The Matrix*. All the lights were out and Tanya sat close to me. Before the evening was over, we were kissing. And it went a bit further than that.

I had not seen Andrea since the night my parents were going to separate. Two more weeks had passed. Late at night, lying in my bed, I wondered about who she was, where she was. Had she been a true figment of my imagination? A hallucination? And such a convincing one at that. Such an interesting and charming one.

The other option was that she had been real — at least as real as any apparition can be — and that she had done her "job." She had helped me with my parents, helped me with Tanya, helped me with me. I was back on track, back on the road to becoming an upper-middle-class consumer-oriented suburbanite like my dad. He had even gone so far already as to buy me my first set of golf clubs. In the backyard, he was coaching me to putt better.

Andrea had conceivably worked these miracles — "fixed" my life and moved on. (To where? To whom?) I tried contacting her — with telepathy — and had no luck. I put myself into self-hypnosis and tried to project out into the world, into the multi-tiered universe to find her, but still no luck.

But why had she been so afraid of coming into my house? Why had she been there in my room and so uncontrollably upset when my dad was leaving? One part of me felt that it was right that I "moved on." My parents may not have solved all their problems but they didn't argue much. They were still pretty busy but made a point of trying to create what my father kept calling "quality time" at home. My mother sold a $600,000 house and the bond market was looking up. So everything was improving.

I knew the drugs changed my day-to-day dealings on so many levels. I continued to miss the old me sometimes. My brain had once been filled with so many images, so many crazy thoughts. Some totally insane, some pure gibberish, some amazing. I had been a visionary, a seer, a wild genius, a maniac, and a lunatic, and now I was a well-groomed teenage boy with the right clothes and a girlfriend. I envisioned the pharmaceutical company that made my drug using me for a TV commercial: before and after. Simon the wonder boy of science. A product of Aldous Huxley's *Brave New World*. Maybe there was no going back.

I sat at my desk in my room and looked at the cardboard box of weird and paranormal files. It all seemed a little childish — the fascinations of a very lonely boy. Each file was of a different colour. In some areas of my life I had always been very organized.

The orange folder was the one I had read over and over and it included articles from magazines and newspapers about right-brain and left-brain research. Split-brain research it was called. The right side of the brain is where the imagination does its work and it's where the creative stuff comes from. The left hemisphere of the brain is associated with logic and language control.

Dr. Roger Sperry at Caltech was a researcher in this area and worked with some mental patients who had actually been treated for epilepsy by severing the ties between the two hemispheres. They were not unlike me — with my bruised and injured brain and my missing connective tissue. It was as if the lines were down between the two halves of the brain. Sperry suggested from his research that severing the ties was like turning someone into two different individuals. That, to me, had always been a scary thought, but I did not see myself as any kind of split personality.

I knew from my own research and piecing things together that I was more right-brained than left. My imagination was powerful — full of all those weird and crazy and wonderful images and ideas. I often thought of myself as intuitive. (*The teacher is going to call on Davis when she turns around*, I would think. And she would.)

Julian Jaynes, another researcher, had figured out that primitive peoples paid more attention to things most people consider to be invisible. They were, like me, more right-brained and more intuitive. They heard things that weren't "there" — auditory hallucinations. They saw things that were not physical — often thought to be ghosts and angels and demons and such. And they often instinctively knew when there was danger or when the weather was about to change dramatically or if a loved one was in trouble — even if at a great distance. All of those qualities were forsaken when we became "civilized" and started to rely on our left hemispheres. Or so the story goes.

So, after I started back in on the meds, I had evolved from primitive to modern man. My guess is that the drug I was taking either suppressed right-brain activity or enhanced left-brain activity. It was a great little chemical experiment going on in my head. Funny though, that for a kid who had such a rich, crazy imagination, I had been so totally organized by keeping these files of paranormal and meta-physical clippings. I looked at the pile of "unprocessed" newspapers and magazines that my mom was now delivering dutifully to my room each day. I was wondering if it might be time to put that all behind me and get on with my new life here in the so-called real world.

A typical evening for me was once sitting alone in my room with my "research" — reading the wacky news items, trying to communicate with the dead, or taking a trip by way of astral projection. That was all behind me, I supposed. Instead, nowadays, if I was home, I would read my school texts, spend time on the phone with Tanya, and, if I wanted to travel, I'd have to take a bus or get a ride from my folks.

Lately I had been wondering about Ozzie. The Ozman, as I had fondly called him. Long gone, for sure, but he had been my best friend, heck my only friend, for so long and then he was gone. We had talked on the phone after he moved to the coast but he'd never come back to visit. And I'd never gone to see him. I pictured him out there on the beach playing volleyball with the girls and hanging out with the surfers. Maybe he had his own board. Maybe, if I found him, he could teach me to surf — just like he had coached me at skateboarding. Ozzie was always there, always the one to say, "Go for it, Simon. Fearless focus." That was his motto: fearless focus.

Ozzie never got hurt. Although he'd always push *me* one step beyond what I had been capable of up to that point. I never blamed him for my accident, though. Never once.

I rifled thought a drawer in my desk where I kept old photos. I remembered Oz as this skinny little kid — not much different from me. We were like two walking coat hangers — thin, all bones, big headed for our physical frames. Oz wore rimless glasses. He had hair that stood straight up. Skin pale as a bar of Ivory soap. No one had a sense of humour like he did. The Ozzer made me laugh.

But not one photo of Ozzie. I did find a couple of old letters from the dude. Nothing recent, just some stuff from way back, not long after he had moved away. He wrote about living right by the beach, about watching people from his window with binoculars, learning to read their lips and being able to tune into their conversations. Odd man Oz, for sure. But there was no return address.

I rooted through my desk some more looking for a phone number. Jeez, I felt bad that I hadn't called my old buddy in a few years now. Maybe it was about time to do just that. But I couldn't find anything with his name on it. No number to call.

In my closet was a model of a DNA molecule that we had made together from blocks of wood. "Deoxyribonucleic acid" had once been our favourite phrase. I remember making the model and painting it; after we received honourable mention at the science fair, Ozzie wanted to pour lighter fluid on it and burn it outside at night. But I had talked him out of it. It was probably the only time I had talked the Oz out of anything.

But no address, no phone number. Maybe I wasn't meant to phone him. There was a good chance he wouldn't like the new me at all.

CHAPTER ELEVEN

And then it was my birthday. Seventeen years old. Tanya met me at my locker and held a piece of mistletoe over my head. "It's not Christmas," I said.

"The Druids didn't have to wait for Christmas." She kissed me hard on the lips in front of everyone. And she slid her tongue into my mouth. It was the Druids who had brought us together, so they were often a part of our intimate conversations.

"After school today, we should go do something special. My treat."

"Let's make a stone circle and worship the sun," I said. "Maybe build a fire and dance naked around it."

"Be serious."

"I am," I teased.

"Let's do something you really want to do."

"Okay, then. There's someone I'd like for you to meet."

"Gotta run," she said as the bell rang. She lifted the mistletoe again and kissed me one more time. Then she pressed it into my hand and headed off down the hall as I stood there watching her, realizing how much I enjoyed just watching the girl walk. As I was turning to put the mistletoe into my locker, I saw something out of the corner of my eye — another girl walking towards me as the crowd of students in the hall was thinning. I turned to focus on her and was sure it was Andrea. I started to run towards her but she turned and went into a classroom and closed the door behind her.

It wasn't my class but I followed her in, stood there at the front of the room looking at the students settling into their seats. No Andrea. I studied the faces of the girls. No, she wasn't here. Everyone was looking at me and some were laughing.

"Wrong room, Simon," Mrs. Evans said. "Need some help finding your class?"

Now everyone laughed. I said nothing, turned, and fled out the door. I stood there for a minute, my heart pounding, wondering why I felt the way I did. There had never been an Andrea, I told myself. But the thought of her had burst like a bubble coming to the surface of my mind. Hadn't she been the one who had planted some suggestion into Tanya's thoughts originally? Wasn't

Andrea responsible for that? And for beginning the truce between my parents at home. And prompting me to take my medication and becoming everything that I was now.

Later that day, Tanya sat in the seat behind me in my History of Civilization class. I could feel her picking lint off the sweater I was wearing. It was rather public and very sweet. A sign of affection, for sure. Her interest and concern for me had grown to something quite extraordinary for a guy who had never had a girlfriend. Sometimes I wondered if it was completely brought on in some weird metaphysical way. Some kind of witchcraft, some kind of mind-altering effect. But who was I to question such a good thing?

I pondered all this as Mr. Holman, quite enthusiastically, lectured about how the barbaric Gauls invaded Rome in 400 B.C. There were no walled fortresses to keep them out and they stormed down from the north, killing, destroying, and spilling more blood into the great thirsty mouth of history itself.

When I was younger and lustily reading many books on psychics and metaphysics, I became a fan of what was once called "automatic writing." Like others before me, some documented by the likes of William James (the so-called father of modern psychology), I would sit at a desk and put myself into a trance and then let my hand travel with a pen over a sheet of paper. And so I sat one day back then, with pen in hand, on a lonely grey winter afternoon, and went out into other realms, waiting for a spirit to enter into me so I would begin writing.

Certainly my hand moved, and I scrawled away for twenty minutes or more at a time, but I could never read what I had written. Fluid loops and curves, Ls and Ts and numbers even, but it was all garbage. This happened at least six times before I focused on a specific request inside my trance.

After relaxing every part of my body and mind, I seemed to travel to some other place where I put out a silent request to anyone listening in that realm that I was looking for an entity (one of my most cherished words in those days) with good handwriting.

And thus it seemed that something entered into me. I could feel "him" occupying my thoughts. I gripped the pen a little tighter, sat more upright, and began to compose words upon the page.

> Here ye, hear ye. Smitten twice all called
> to the kingdom of Dilapades and hence-
> forth wisdom to the ponds and forests.
> Gentle composure towns slipping east all
> afternoon whilst crown grumble folk
> meet between. Fumble stock over the
> drumlin. Twin earth power root and

mangle foot. Alms to all the sad armies
beneath the cataracts. Lessons one two
three. Dream wild little boy thimble
high and carry wide. Allegiance to all the
winged thoughts. Adieu.

I remember falling asleep after writing that and
dreamed of wide, green, rolling fields with a castle in
the distance. A lone white horse came out to greet me
and stood shyly by my side nibbling at the grass. I woke
when my mother knocked on my door, telling me it was
time for dinner.

For many days I studied what he or I had written. I
had succeeded in contacting or conjuring a spirit with
excellent penmanship but I wasn't sure he made any
sense. I read meaning into every part of it though and
memorized it, reciting it to Ozzie as we rode our skateboards along the paved bike path down by the river.
Ozzie was most impressed and urged me to recite it at
the school talent night saying it was a poem I had "written." Well, I had written it, but it wasn't exactly mine.

I did, in fact, recite my "poem" before a rather
stunned audience of parents, students, and teachers. I
was in grade six at the time. Adults, many of them, told
me they were amazed at my gift. They thought it was a
fabulous poem and they acted as if they understood
what it meant. All except for one old geezer — a retired

English professor who introduced himself as Dr. Lester Willis. He took me aside after the show and accused me of plagiarism. "You lifted it from James Joyce, didn't you, lad?" There was a musty smell about him and an odd look in his eyes.

"No. I don't even know who James Joyce is."

He became quite rude and nasty. "Theft of any sort, especially great literature, is a crime against humanity. My guess is you copied this from *Ulysses*, or possibly *Finnegan's Wake*. Am I correct?"

I had heard of neither book, although I looked them up later in the library and found them dense and unreadable but not entirely unlike my "poem."

"Sir," I said, "I did have some help in writing it."

"Very well," he said, changing demeanour, now satisfied. "Then you have confessed. The truth will always prevail."

He turned away, and it suddenly struck me how oddly he was dressed. I never saw him again and thought it strange that a man like that would have been in attendance at all. It was as if he himself had come from another time and another place. A restless literary constable on the prowl for boys claiming to have written verse that was not their own.

My parents typically had not been able to attend the evening and thus missed my moment of glory. My father picked me up afterwards, however, and at home my mother asked to read the poem. I could tell from her furrowed brow that she feared this to be another example of how odd a child I truly was. I did not 'fess up to the origin of the work.

"The handwriting is extraordinary," she said.

There were many more days of scrawling, rolling, tumbling, florid handwriting on white pages but there were no real words to speak of. Vowels and consonants strung together but mostly just hills and valleys of ink, Vs and Ss and endless Ms. In my trance, I would request contact with someone who could write in English, someone with good penmanship, and someone who had something intelligent to say.

These seemed to be fairly stiff demands. The "poet" never returned to me. There was a feminine entity that drew pictures of flowers with bees buzzing about them. And a pale boy with spiky hair who drew kites. And then it all stopped and each time I tried to hypnotize myself I just fell asleep.

I explained to Tanya where I wanted to go.

"She's a what?"

"A psychic," I said. "And an old friend. Her name is Lydia, and she's unusual. I want you to like her."

"I thought we were going to do something special. It's your birthday, remember?"

"This is special. Lydia says she has a new, um, guide."

"Like a guide dog? Is she blind?"

"No. Lydia is a medium. She contacts spirits, dead people. Sometimes they can speak through her."

"This is giving me the creeps. Can we maybe do something else?"

"Be brave, Tanya. It's no big deal. I don't know if I believe in any of it. But this is important to me."

"All right," she said, but I could tell she would rather be going to the mall.

I knocked first and then we walked up the stairs and in through the open door to Lydia's apartment. Lydia was sitting at the kitchen table smoking a joint. A thin ribbon of smoke, like a pale wispy wraith, drifted towards the ceiling. In front of her, spread out on the table as if it had just been spilled, was maybe a quarter ounce of marijuana leaves and buds. Behind her was a large mirror on the wall that made the room seem like it was much larger than it was. It also had the unnerving quality of making you spend too much time looking at yourself while you were talking to Lydia.

Lydia smiled when she saw me and waved us in. I closed the door behind us. Tanya took my hand and looked a little scared. Lydia was holding in a hit of smoke she had just inhaled. Her glasses were a little fogged up. The room smelled of the powerful combination of weed and garlic and lavender.

Lydia exhaled a small nimbus cloud and motioned for us to sit down. She stubbed out her joint in an ashtray, talking to it. "I'll finish you later," she said. "Don't go away." She took a deep breath as if she'd been deprived of oxygen and then looked up at us. "His name is Montague," she said.

"Your new guide?"

"Yes. He's a bit of a snob. Seventeenth-century upper-crust English. Quite the aristocrat. Opinionated, blustery at times, but well-informed, and once you get past the surface, he has a good heart."

"How did you find him?" I asked.

"He found me," Lydia said. "He knew I was drifting. No anchor, no sail, no rudder. Just drifting. Who's your friend?"

"Tanya, Lydia. Lydia, Tanya."

"Your parents give her to you for your birthday?" Lydia asked. I was surprised that she knew it was my birthday.

Tanya looked insulted.

"It was a joke," Lydia explained and looked directly into her eyes. She nodded at me. "Did he tell you he saved my ass in the Napoleonic Wars? And did he tell you he is a healer? He's not using it now, but he is. Look at his hands sometime. Look closely. There is a tremendous amount of healing energy in this one. But he doesn't know what to do with it yet. He will eventually. You watch for it."

Tanya was feeling quite uncomfortable, I could tell. She was way outside her comfort zone. I was wondering if I had made a big mistake coming here with her.

"I'm glad you kids are here. And forgive me for the smoke. It's herbal, I assure you. Pure organic. Nothing to be afraid of here. Everything that happens here is just smoke and mirrors. Hocus pocus. Something some of us do to keep ourselves entertained." She waved away the smoke in the air and turned to make a funny face into the mirror. She was trying, in her own odd way, to make Tanya feel more comfortable.

Lydia pointed to the leaves and buds on the table-top. "This is a variation of reading tea leaves in the bottom of a cup. I study the random patterns here and receive a few messages about the future. Stay quiet for a minute and let's see."

Tanya squirmed beside me. Silently mouthed, "Let's go," but I squeezed her hand gently.

"Something terrible is going to happen in Europe," she said. "Something political. In a city. A big city." She was pointing with her forefinger to a cluster of leaves. "And I think things will get worse in Africa, especially in the sub-Sahara, before it gets any better."

She pointed to another part of the table. "All the interest in Mars will turn out to be a waste of time. Money should have gone to health care, not space. The queen will make an important announcement before the year is over. Small wars, too. Many of them but nothing big." Suddenly she looked up and smiled at Tanya. "Listen up, honey," she said. "This will be on the test." And then she laughed.

I'm not sure why she said that, but Tanya recognized it as a kind of direct insult. That had been the question Tanya was famous for at school. At least one teacher had made fun of her for saying it, and she had cut it out, but I don't think I had ever mentioned anything about it to Lydia.

"Excuse me, kids. I have to pee. Be right back." Lydia cleaned up the pot on the table and brushed it with a hairbrush into a jewellery box. Then she left the room.

"I'm gonna leave," Tanya said. "I don't like any of this."

"She's harmless," I said. "Please stay."

But she shook her head. "I'll talk to you later."

"I'll call you," I said.

"Sure," she said, then got up and walked out of the apartment.

Tanya was one of the better things that had happened in my life and I expected that one day she would move on from me for some better looking guy. She was the first girl I had ever kissed. She was the first for a lot of things, and maybe I should have apologized to Lydia and followed her. But I didn't.

Lydia returned and noticed Tanya had left but didn't mention it. "All our lives liquids just flow through us," she said. "I drink my tea and it sustains me and then what's left, which is most of it, I just piss it out and away it goes. Have you ever thought about these cycles of things, Simon?"

"Sure. Water. Food. Money. My parents try too hard to get money but they don't even keep it. It flows through them."

"Water. Food. Money. Smoke. Ideas. But it works on other levels too. Time flows through you. Today you are seventeen but tomorrow you'll be, what? Seventy. Time will continue to flow. You through it, it through you. But you didn't come here for this. It's your birthday and I'm sorry I insulted your friend. I meant to, but I didn't mean to. If you know what I mean."

"It's okay, I think."

"You're not thinking about her, though. Which is odd. You are thinking about another girl," Lydia ventured.

"I am. That's why I came."

I explained about going back on the medication.

Lydia knew my past. She knew about the weird stuff I did as a little kid and then about the accident.

"I'm going to contact Montague. You're not telling me everything, I know, but you must have a reason for that. Give me your wallet." She set out a great chunk of amethyst crystal in front of her and waved her hand over it.

I handed her my wallet, and she held it between her hands and closed her eyes. She had lost a lot of potential customers this way. *Give me your wallet*, she would say, or *your ring*, or *your watch*. She claimed she needed something that a person wore or carried or kept close to their body. She said it carried a "signature of their vibrations." For Lydia, vibrations had a lot to do with everything. The amethyst was good for focusing the vibrations, she said.

"Take a deep breath, Simon, and relax. You're just along for the ride. But Montague is playing hard to get." I watched her eyes moving beneath her closed lids as if she were searching the darkness for her guide. Suddenly she yawned.

"Okay. Found him. I'm going to try to tell you what Montague has to say and you can ask a question or make a comment and we'll see where it goes. Okay?"

"Okay," I said.

What I was doing there, if I was to be honest with myself, was trying to verify if Andrea was at all real or purely something I had made up in my head. I didn't trust myself. I didn't trust Andrea. I had no clear reference points. No one else saw her. If Lydia could somehow contact her or at least provide some evidence ... well, this was not hard science. This was the best I could do. I needed some guidance. Who better to take it from than a seventeenth-century aristocratic snob?

"Montague says that if you want him to help you, you have to show him a bit more respect."

"Sorry," I said.

"He accepts your apology. Now he wants to know about the four women in your life. He sees four."

"There's Tanya."

"We know about Tanya," Lydia said. "She's not why you are here."

"There's, well, my mother."

"Maybe she's the one."

"What do you mean, the one?"

"The one with the problem. Who else?"

I wasn't sure what to say next. "There's you, Lydia. You've known me longer than just about anyone."

"I don't think this is about me but it could be. Hmm. No, Montague says, it's not about me. Now he's reminding me I should take more vitamins, eat more vegetables. He says you aren't getting enough roughage, either. He says he's sorry to divert like this but can't help himself. He's a health food nut in his own seventeenth-century way. Root vegetables, he's big on. And Brussels sprouts. He wants to know if you eat them."

"No."

"That's a mistake, he says. You should. Tell him you'll increase your roughage, drink more water, and eat root vegetables and then we can move on."

"I promise," I said. "I'll start today."

"Great. Now we can move on." Her eyes were still closed. She waved her hand over the crystal and put it back on top of the wallet.

"The fourth woman?" I asked.

"He says he doesn't know yet. He sees four directions. North, south, east, and west. A woman is an anchor at each point in your life. I am the east. I've always been the east, so that takes care of me. I am the sunrise, the birds in the morning sky. The east wind."

I wasn't sure I was following her and wondered if she or Montague were just teasing me, wasting my time. Not that I had anything more important to do.

"Your mother is north. She is a good person but has coldness about her. No, that's a bit cruel. She has a reserve that often holds her back from telling you how much she loves you. She is troubled but better now than before. I think it was you who somehow helped her."

"And Tanya?"

"Tanya is south. Sensual. Sweet in some ways. Weak in

other ways. She has some growing up to do. Her world is small. She's like a small tropical greenhouse. Contained. Limited for now. But she is not the one with the problem."

"What about west?" I asked.

Lydia turned my wallet over in her hand.

"Montague wants to know why you are holding back."

"Because I need to know something. And if I reveal too much, I may not get the answer I need."

"Chess."

"What?"

"You play chess, right?"

"Sure."

"Montague says you should never sacrifice your queen."

"I don't understand."

"Pawns, rooks, knights, bishops even. But to win by sacrificing the queen is not the thing for a gentleman to do."

"I'll remember that," I said, although I did not fully understand the reference.

"Who rescued you when you were feeling lost?"

"I don't know."

"She did," Lydia answered. "Montague said it was her. West."

"I don't understand what west is."

"West is the setting sun. West is where the day goes.

Time moves in that direction. West is night. Completion. West is death."

I felt a chill run down my spine. I looked into the mirror now behind Lydia and stared at my own face. I am not a mirror person and hardly ever took a look at myself in a mirror. There he was. Me. Seventeen years old today.

"I want you to tell me if she is real," I said. "I need it to come from someone who does not know what I know. Someone who hasn't seen what I've seen."

"Why do you need this so badly?"

"Because this is important to me."

"Montague is feeling annoyed. He wants to know why you are testing him, testing us both."

"It's not you. I'm testing me. I'm testing what I believed to be real. Tell me one thing you know about her. About West."

Lydia frowned. "Montague says you are just a boy. You aren't ready for this. You aren't prepared. He thinks you should just back away from it all. Stay on the path you are on."

"Okay. Is that it?"

"There is no *it*, Montague says. No easy answer. He says, if you are so poorly prepared, maybe you *should* just sacrifice your queen and win your little game and you won't have to worry yourself anymore."

I was feeling frustrated and angry now. At Lydia or Montague or this whole crazy afternoon. I felt a little dizzy. Maybe it was all the marijuana smoke in the room. I was feeling confused and light-headed. I looked at my reflection. Smoke and mirrors. A crazy woman playing tricks with my mind. A dope-smoking, unemployed nutcase entertaining herself. When I took my wallet back, would I find its contents, a single twenty-dollar bill, missing?

Lydia opened her eyes suddenly. "We're through," she said, sliding my wallet back to me. "Montague's gone. I'm feeling tired." She had changed entirely. "I don't think you were fair about this," she said accusingly.

"Maybe I expected too much."

"You wanted answers. You wanted someone to tell you what to do. This is what people want when they come here. They want easy answers, and it usually doesn't work out that way. You have a problem on your hands. You need to decide what to do. You can walk away from it. That's what Montague was telling you, but that's only because you pissed him off. I don't think you can walk away from it."

I sat silently for a minute. Lydia opened a window and began to put dirty cups and saucers into the dishwater in the sink. She squirted in some dish detergent.

Looking out the window now she said this: "It isn't really *her* trying to save you. It's the other way around. You have to save her."

"But I don't even know where she is."

"Then you better find her. Does she have a name?"

"Andrea," I said.

"Well. That wasn't so hard, was it?"

CHAPTER TWELVE

My parents were never good at birthday parties, and this one was no exception. Ice cream. Cake. I blew out the candles. They gave me a bunch of presents I didn't particularly need or want.

My present to myself was flushing my pills down the toilet. I don't know what results I was expecting, but I was becoming more confused over who I liked best. The old me, the new me, or just me.

Tanya called while I was out for a walk but I didn't call her back. I wasn't quite prepared for it if she had bad news for me — the spell had worn off, maybe. I had turned back into a pumpkin. She had been totally freaked out by Lydia. Did I really want such a straitlaced girl?

Or maybe she just wanted to apologize. It seemed that I had to choose allegiance, loyalty to one of two girls. Tanya was the prettier of the two, but was I that shallow? Maybe. But then Tanya was real and Andrea was ... exactly what?

So Andrea was west. She was death. She was my queen. All metaphorically speaking. I knew that whatever Lydia was up to with her weirdness and her so-called spirit guides, it was up to me to interpret what she told me. But if it was all a chess game, then who was my opponent? And how was I doing? Winning or losing?

I looked at the pile of newspapers sitting by my desk. Maybe it was time to put all that behind me. If I wanted to research anything, I could use the Internet. Did I really want to spend more evenings alone in my room with a pair of scissors? I moved the pile of newspapers over towards the door. I'd haul them down later and put them with the recycling.

In doing so, I knocked over my research box and a folder spilled its contents on the floor. Witchcraft. I hadn't thought about witchcraft for quite a while, although it had once been up there in my top ten most important subjects of interest. Ozzie was convinced witches were real and had always wanted to meet one. We had theories about who they were. Certainly our fourth grade teacher, Mrs. Dexter. She could paralyze you with her stare or make you feel ten feet tall with her smile.

Ozzie and I assumed that witchcraft was an honourable undertaking for the most part but there were probably a few nasty witches around too. The only test we had heard of was one we could obviously never use. It was the ancient one of throwing a suspected witch into a pond. If she floated, she was a witch. If she sank, then not. Probably many non-witches had drowned over the years in such ponds and the floaters mostly were stoned or hanged or burned to death. Our ancestors were not particularly tolerant of women with unusual abilities.

If a woman could cure your wart, for example, you might be thankful and give her a loaf of homemade pumpernickel bread, but then if a neighbour heard about this, he might accuse her of being a witch. And then the dirty work began.

My witchcraft file contained mostly stuff I'd photocopied from books since there was not a lot of news about witches in any of the local papers. I reread an article I had about an accused witch during the reign of King James I in England. Poor Gilly Duncan, a servant girl from North Berwick, had a gift for healing and, as a reward for her kind deeds, the local authorities accused her of being a witch and having sex with the devil. She was tortured and "confessed," leading to her being burned to death. Such stories were repeated for centuries.

The death penalty for witches remained until 1736 in England, but it remained illegal to call yourself a witch in that country until 1951. In another time, Lydia certainly would have been considered a witch. She was an avowed pagan and believed in her herbs and spirits.

I put the folder away in my "research box" right between werewolves and wormholes. And I walked out into the night. I needed some exercise. I wanted to clear my head and figure out what I was going to do about Andrea — if I was going to do anything at all. I walked west into the night.

It was a clear night, and the sky was full of stars. I saw one shooting star and could locate at least two satellites. Venus was low on the horizon, and I think I could see Mars. I would stop near streetlights and peer into the shadows behind trees and parked cars. I think I expected Andrea to appear, to walk out of the darkness and come back into my life. But she did nothing of the sort.

When I arrived back home, I heard my parents arguing again. So much for the truce. I listened long enough to determine that they were arguing about money this time, not about me. I wondered if I could find a modern-day witch to cast a spell and make them stop arguing, make them like each other a little more. I wondered if Andrea could use those influences she had used on Tanya to help my parents. And so I continued to ponder this problem of Andrea. Did she exist, and was she in trouble? What kind of trouble could it be? And how could I possibly help?

I was right about Tanya. She was mad at me. I found her in the hallway at school. "That Lydia lady made my skin crawl. Why did you take me there?"

"I thought you would find it interesting."

"You don't believe any of her crap, do you?"

"I like to keep an open mind," I said.

"Why didn't you call me back last night?"

And then I said something that I would quickly regret. "I don't know. I guess I didn't think it was important."

Early on in life you figure out that some very ordinary words can mean many different things to different people. What I had meant was I didn't think it was important to call her back right then, when my head was filled with other things, when I was confused. What she heard me say (reading between the lines and drawing her own conclusions) was that I was saying she wasn't important, that I didn't care, that I was totally uncaring and insensitive.

She gave me a look that shocked me. I saw hurt first but it quickly morphed into anger. "Don't worry," she said. "You won't have to talk to me again." And she walked away.

"Tanya, wait," were the words that came out of my mouth, but they didn't do any good at all.

And it was while I was watching her walk away down the school hallway that I suddenly realized what I was losing. I knew I would not get her back. I had been dreaming about Tanya for a long time. She had allowed me into her life, and I had walked in. She liked me. She was maybe falling in love with me. I think she really was. It had been the most amazing thing.

And now she was walking out of my life, and I had let it happen. I knew instinctively there was no way to repair the damage. And then I was leaning against someone's locker, my head down, and I was sobbing. Something powerful and terrible was sweeping over me. I had not felt anything like this before. I didn't understand it and I couldn't control it. I knew I had to get out of there, so I ran down the hall and outside. I ran long and hard down the school driveway and down the road until I came to the old railway tracks that led into the woods. My chest was heaving and my eyes burned. I thought I heard a voice calling to me, but when I turned there was no one there.

I sat down by the river and watched the water, studied the patterns of light and dark, the ripple effect on the surface. I remembered being here with Andrea. I remembered walking here with Tanya. How different they were. Now they had both come into my life and both disappeared. And I wished that I had never known either one. There was a cold hollow place inside me, and it was growing larger. I took a deep breath and tried to focus on being calm, but I began to feel a throbbing pain in my head.

I wished for a kind and healing witch to walk out of those woods and comfort me. But I had no such luck. And I was feeling terribly, horribly alone. Isolated. I did not want to go home. I couldn't bring myself to go back to school. I thought I heard someone call my name again, a nickname I hadn't heard for a long while. "Slime-on."

No one there. Trees. Vines. Wind moving things around a little. I looked back at the water, at the reflection of me shifting and rippling on the dark surface. And then in the reflection, someone standing behind me. A kid. Ozzie.

The image came into sudden clarity and it was perfectly clear. He was standing there, smiling. And he still had a skateboard in his hand. And he still looked to be twelve years old.

"Ozzie," I said out loud, but when I turned around no one was there.

One of my science teachers had told us once about the principle of Occam's razor, which stated that, usually, the best explanation for any unusual phenomena is the simplest one. If ever there was a time to put Occam's razor to the task of cutting through the complexity of things to look for the simplest explanation, it was now. Ozzie was the same age as me and living a two-hour drive away in a home near the ocean. While we had not kept in touch, it was not possible that he still looked like the wiry little rat that he had been back during our reckless skateboard days.

Stress can cause both visual and auditory hallucinations, the experts say. And I had sure experienced plenty of stress, worrying about my parents and now getting dumped by Tanya. I had also flushed the pills that were intended in part to "keep me in balance." I believed then that the combination of the two factors must have sent me off the deep end. I suddenly realized that I could remember everything about Ozzie from before my accident and nothing about him after it.

I walked home, both frazzled and uncertain as to what I might see next or do next. I went to my room, and inside I tripped over the pile of newspapers I had failed to get rid of. I did not look in the mirror. In fact, I put a shirt over it. I drank a large glass of water and searched my desk drawer for some leftover pills, but I had been thorough. I was chemical free and stuck with that fact. I could not tell my parents about the missing pills. They would know I had chucked them. I'd done that before. To them, it would be a sign that I was still in trouble. (And I was, but I didn't want them to know.)

I could feel all of my energy draining out of my body, seeping out of the soles of my feet and into the floor. I lay down on my bed and I faded into a deep sleep.

In my dream, Tanya came back to me and I apologized. But Tanya had changed. She was both Andrea and Tanya — fused. Well, dreams are not meant to be logical. But she seemed one and the same and I seemed to accept that just fine. We were standing on a grassy island in the middle of a four-lane highway. It was noisy from the traffic and I could smell exhaust. And I kept saying that we should get to the other side. On one side was a city and on the other side of the highway was the sea. There was a boardwalk there and beyond it the blue, perfect ocean. I assumed we were trying to get to the beach even though we didn't look like we were dressed for it.

There was no break in traffic at all, and Andrea/ Tanya kept saying that all we had to do was start walking and the cars would stop. But I kept pulling her back. And each time she looked at me her face had somehow changed. Tanya smiling. Andrea putting her finger to her lips. Tanya angry with me. Andrea with that terrified look. Finally, as she turned away, she pulled me out into the onslaught of traffic. I heard screeching tires and then I woke up.

It was five-thirty in the afternoon and my father had just pulled his car into the driveway. I drank some more water and changed my clothes. I tested one quick look in the mirror and saw that I looked like hell. A quick shower made me appear semi-human, but both my parents said that they thought I looked a bit ill at dinner.

"Simon, you spend too much time inside. How about if you and I go to the beach this Saturday?" my father said. He was not inviting my mother, just me.

I stirred my food with my fork. "I'd like that," I said. "And maybe we can visit Ozzie. I haven't seen the guy in a really long time."

My parents looked at each other and then back at me. My mother changed the subject. "I got a bid on that new listing but it was way under the asking price. And the buyer asked me to trim my commission fee. I told him to stuff it where the sun doesn't shine."

"That was tactful of you," my father said.

Friday I stayed home from school. I explained to my parents that it was a matter of too much stress. "I just need to chill for a day."

I moved that pile of newspapers back towards my desk and clipped a few oddities about Elvis appearances, sign language communication with apes, and a magician named Gabor who many claimed could make household appliances float in mid-air — blenders, toasters, microwave ovens. He did not make people or animals float, he said, because it was against his principles. He also said this: "Magic is when there is an effect with no apparent cause. All of my effects, my magic, occur because I make it happen. The observer simply does not have the ability to see the forces I use." As if that explained it. I wondered if he was the real thing or just another showman who made things appear to happen through gimmicks and visual tricks.

I turned on my computer and found an opponent online to test my skills at chess. He won three games before I realized my demise each time was the result of my attempts to protect my queen with little regard for the loss of other strategic pieces. I logged off and noted my stress levels rising again as I began to blame myself for losing Tanya. But even more than that, I was worried about Andrea, that amazing person who had come into my life, stayed so briefly, and then vanished.

If each of us could peer into the future, we would alter a considerable amount of the things we do in the present. We would be different people for sure. Gabor's simple statement got me thinking about cause and effect. His explanation of magic could apply to many things. If every morning you hear a sound like two claps of thunder at exactly nine-thirty you think that is odd. It is unlikely that it can be thunder since such things don't happen on a daily schedule. You run through many possibilities but come to the conclusion that it is inexplicable — some odd phenomena that appears to have no logical cause. Since the sound has no negative effects and no particular positive ones, after a while most folks would just stop thinking about it or, at most, find it mildly amusing each time it occurs.

Let's say, later, much later, you discover that an overseas supersonic flight to Paris is passing over where you live at nine-thirty each morning. And it clicks. The plane is breaking the sound barrier overhead and that is what you are hearing. You now have a theory, and ultimately an explanation of the cause of the effect. But if you had not been alerted to the information, by chance or intention, then you would continue to assume that the sound was a strange phenomenon — a kind of magic.

Lydia had guided me through several possibilities of what she called "divining" my future. She was a hardcore horoscope believer and argued that even Carl Jung, the famous psychologist, was a believer in the possibility of using astrology to tap into some kind of code as to how our lives are played out according to a pattern that includes stars and planets and galaxies.

She was lukewarm on palmistry but thought it had some merit. I told her I didn't like the look of my lifeline and she studied it herself and frowned. "I've known ninety-year-old men whose lifelines peter out to nothing in the middle of their palm. Yours doesn't end. It's broken off and begins again. There." She traced the crease that began just below my forefinger and carved a deep canal across my hand and down around the pad of my thumb towards my wrist.

Lydia was always more interested in what she called "the forces at work within you and the energy around you." She'd say, "When the planets are in your favour, move forward. When they are against you, retreat."

I was clearly in retreat, but I wanted to know if *I* was the cause of my own effect or if it was something external. Not necessarily planets, but something else at work. I felt like my life was this great, crazy, sometimes amusing, sometimes impossible jigsaw puzzle. I was unable to fit enough of the pieces of the puzzle together to grasp what the picture was supposed to be when completed. And I was pretty sure that I was missing a number of key pieces.

This is why I rather wished I could look ahead into the future and return to the present with a clear vision as to what I should do next. What was it I was supposed to do?

Aside from the usual methods of palmistry, astrology, Tarot cards, and throwing the I Ching, Lydia told me that down through the ages there had been a lot of pretty wacky ways of attempting to foretell the future. Alomancy was a method using salt. Antropomancy was reading the future by studying the entrails of human sacrifices (a rather extreme method, one would assume). Necromancy was the old standby of listening to what the dead have to tell you about the future. Alectryomancy involved simply throwing down some corn on tiles of letters from the alphabet. Then you let your favourite rooster peck away and see what words he spells that will prophesy what tomorrow may bring. One method called xenomancy involved divination by interpreting the appearance of foreign visitors. I had a feeling that none of the above was going to be suitable for my dilemma.

There would be no easy way to prepare myself for what tomorrow may bring. And looking back, I am sure now that nothing could have prepared me for what was to come next.

CHAPTER THIRTEEN

I was really hoping that my father would drive me to the coast on Saturday as he'd promised. I believed that simply looking at the sea would help fix my head. I didn't think he'd go along with my great lifelong desire to learn how to surf. But I figured he would at least help me try to locate the Oz.

I dug out some old letters from my long-lost buddy, but not one of them had an address. He had moved to the shore town of Whitby but that was all I knew. I tried phoning information for a listing of his father, Winston Coleman. There was a W. Coleman but that was all. I tried phoning W. Coleman, but it turned out to be an elderly woman named Winnie who must not have had many people to talk to because she wanted to tell me about her cat and the skin allergies it had.

I did an Internet search for Ozzie Coleman, Winston Coleman, and Ozzie's mother, whose first name was very vague, but I was fairly sure it was Lizzie. So I tried Lizzie Coleman, Elizabeth Coleman, Liz Coleman, and E. Coleman. Nothing.

I phoned Whitby High School and explained about my quest for an old friend. At first the secretary said no way, but I pleaded, so she put me through to a school counsellor.

"It doesn't ring any bells," he said, trying to be helpful. "Hang on."

He did a quick search and then told me that there were two Colemans in the school, both girls. No Ozzie. "His family probably just moved on, maybe back while he was still in junior high. I don't have access to any records there. A lot of families move in and out of this town. How long has it been since you've seen him?"

"Four years," I said.

"Sorry I can't be more helpful. Keep looking. You'll probably find him. Good luck."

My own prediction that my father would find an excuse to bow out of the trip to the beach at Whitby proved faulty. We were actually on the road Saturday morning, my father with a big mug of coffee and me looking out the window.

My dad turned down the radio. "About this thing you want to do ... track down your friend ..."

"Ozzie," I said. "You remember him. I know you always thought he was trouble but he was my friend." I had this feeling that the Ozman was part of that puzzle that was my life. He was one of the missing pieces. And that somehow, I didn't know how, he would be able to help me figure out how to get in touch with Andrea. Ozzie always, even way back when we were kids, had the ability to make the leap of faith that made it seem that anything was possible.

My father put on his sunglasses and cleared his throat to speak again, but I interrupted.

"We can try the library, maybe a couple of skate-board shops. I'm sure that if we are real polite and go to a police station, if it's a slow day with no major crime, someone will try to help. It's really important to me."

"Okay," he said, giving a great sigh. "If it's that important. You won't mind if I just hang back and wait in the car?"

I smiled. Just like him to *not* want to get involved, but at least he was driving me to Whitby. I was certain I was going to find Ozzie. Reunion time.

But by three o'clock, I gave up the search. Every place I went to I had been the most polite seventeen-year-old on the planet. Even the cops tried to be helpful, but I had no luck at all. I knew Ozzie's father had been some kind of computer salesman so I even tried calling the computer stores from the yellow pages.

"Let's go to the beach," my father finally said.

I had given it my best shot and was feeling pretty low. If Ozzie had moved, why hadn't he at least let me know where he had gone? I began to wonder if something awful might have happened to him or his family.

My father parked, we got out, and we walked onto the beach. What had started out as a sunny day had turned overcast. Dark thunderclouds hung over us and the sea looked dense and brooding. There was not a breath of wind. The beach had emptied, and we walked the sand down to the edge of the water. A few surfers were still out there, far from shore, catching waves and riding across long glassy walls of water. It looked different from what I had imagined.

My father took off his sunglasses. "I guess I don't need these." He stood there beside me looking out to sea.

I didn't say anything, although I felt bad that I had wasted most of the day in my failed search instead of spending some "quality time" with my father. Then he dropped the bombshell.

"Simon," he said. "There was no Ozzie. He never existed. He was someone you made up in your head."

I felt nauseous just then. I couldn't understand why he would say a thing like this.

"You remember your accident?"

"Yes. And I know you blamed Ozzie for it, right? It's true that he was there, but it was my stupid decision."

My father rubbed his face and took a deep breath. "Ozzie was your imaginary friend from the time you were a little kid. At first we thought it was cute and that he would just eventually go away." He waved his hands in the air. "In fact, I guess we wanted to believe that you knew he was just that, an imaginary friend."

"Why are you saying this? I know Ozzie was real."

"He wasn't. When you started doing crazy things, your mother and I were truly getting worried. We had taken you to get professional help. This was before the accident. Do you remember that?"

"No."

"Dr. Waller?"

"You're the one imagining things."

"I'm not. After the accident you suffered some memory loss, so it's understandable that you don't remember some things. And you changed. You were different. And there were complications."

"I know all that," I said, feeling anxious now, unsettled. More stress creeping me out.

"You kept asking about Ozzie. It was the accident itself or the medication you were on, but either way,

Ozzie simply wasn't there anymore for you. So we told you he had moved away."

"But I have letters."

My father put his hands up in the air. "You always had a powerful imagination."

I was shaking now, and my father put his arm around me. My friend Ozzie had been as real to me as anything had ever been in my life.

It began to rain, and I watched one final lone surfer catch a wave, stand, cruise across a long dark wall of water as lightning flashed behind him, striking the sea far in the distance. He rode the wave in and then came ashore. He walked right past us, but we must have been such a sorry looking pair standing there on the beach that he stopped. My father asked, "How is it out there?"

"Awesome," he replied. "I'm beat, though. Been in the water three hours. My arms are noodled and my skin is pruned. But it was worth it." He looked at me and I felt like I recognized him. I expected he was going to hold out his hand and pour skateboard ball bearings into mine, but he just said, "Ever try it?"

"No," I said.

"Takes a while to learn, but once you got it, it's yours for life. Take it easy."

My dad smiled. We turned and followed the surfer off the beach, got in our car, and began to drive home. It began to rain. Halfway there, I was feeling pretty depressed. My father was trying to make small talk, telling me about his job, but I wasn't listening. I was nodding off when something made me turn around.

And there she was. A girl lying down in the back-seat, asleep. Andrea.

She did not wake up and, filled with my own self-doubts, I couldn't bring myself to test the reality of her presence in any way. I was angry with my father for his insane insistence that Ozzie had never existed. He had been part of my young life for years. We had shared so much together. If he was not real, then nothing could be trusted.

My parents had never had a good word to say about Oz, never invited him to stay for dinner, never gone out of their way to be friendly to him. They had always insisted he was somehow "bad" for me. And they were very happy when he was gone. Both my dad and my mom, in my estimation, had told me some ridiculous things to me over the years, given me bad advice, shown me how little they truly understood important things like skateboarding and astral projection and science fiction. They wasted the days of their lives chasing money.

I always hoped to show them that there was another way to live. I wanted to show them they were wrong about so many things. I always knew that I was not normal, that I had problems, but I also knew that I was capable of seeing a kind of wonder in the world. When it came to the occult and the mystical — and the world of the possible — I was endlessly curious. And my mind was always open despite the gargantuan effort of the adult world to get me back on track, to turn me into a clone of my father.

Damn him for saying this to me today. To remove Ozzie from my life, to cut him out with a scalpel, was to amputate a big part of who I was.

All of this was going through my mind there in the car. Pretending to look behind at something we had passed, I turned twice to see if she was still there. She was. Andrea still lay sleeping, and it seemed certain that if my father had turned, he would have been shocked to see an unknown girl back there.

We had not locked the car while we were on the beach. There was nothing inside to steal, and my father's theory was that an unlocked car with a window partially down would attract no thief. A locked car tempted a hoodlum to smash the window with a rock and steal whatever guarded treasure lay inside. Car alarm or no car alarm. These days, no one paid any attention to car alarms. They went off all the time by accident and were a general annoyance. If someone wants to steal your briefcase or your car, they do it one way or the other.

My father stopped to buy us hamburgers, and I insisted we go through the drive-through and eat in the car. I didn't want to leave the car for fear she would be gone when we returned. Given the difficulties of the day, he was not about to say no. We ate silently in the parking lot, and when my dad went inside to use the bathroom, I waited until he was out of sight.

"Andrea, wake up," I said. I touched her hand, and then tapped on it lightly. Nothing.

"Please, Andrea." I reached back and touched her face. I smoothed the hair out of her eyes. I leaned back and listened to the sound of her breathing, felt the warm air on my cheek. I almost kissed her, but I stopped myself. If she was not prepared to wake, she must be exhausted, and I would let her sleep.

Although I had known her only for such a short time, I had sorely missed her when she was gone. I wanted her to stay in my life this time. From now on, I decided, I would try to be attentive to what she needed, rather than what I needed. Andrea was the chessboard queen that I would not sacrifice for my own well-being.

Even though Andrea had always been invisible to everyone but me, I had this sudden fear that when my father returned, he would see her there and I would have to explain. But I was wrong. He was in a hurry to get back on the road and just started up the car and we drove on. He seemed in a great hurry to get home now, as if his effort to tell me that Ozzie was a fairy tale had totally taxed his nerves.

And then she awoke.

"Don't turn around," she whispered. I could feel her breath this time in my ear.

I didn't flinch.

"Your father loves you, Simon. So does your mother. They have their share of problems, but hang onto them. Don't push them away." She sounded very, very tired as if the words took a great effort.

Stay with me. Don't leave again, I wanted to say to her, but I knew if I said anything out loud, my father would freak. I sat staring silently at the road ahead.

"I would stay if I could," she said, answering my silent request. "I'm not sure I can. I'm sorry it didn't work out with Tanya. But there will be others."

I wanted to tell her how much I needed her. I felt a deep connection to this girl. I felt alone in the world without her.

"No one is ever truly alone," she said. "Now stop worrying about me and stay focused on the people around you. I'm going to help your father say what he really feels. It would be nice if you could be kind to him." Then she sat back, and I waited.

"Simon," my father began, "I'm sorry that today didn't turn out better — for both of us. I feel like I haven't always been there for you. I think there's time for us yet, though. You know, sometimes at work, I feel like I don't have a single friend in the world. I'm in competition with everyone in the office. I can survive at my job as long as I can compete. As long as I make the good pitch, sell what I have to sell. Cripes. It's a game, all of it. But it's also plenty serious." The words were spilling out of him, and it wasn't like he was talking to me, his son. More like he was talking to a friend.

"But you're good at what you do, right?" I assured him.

"I'm good enough to hang on. For now. But if I lose my edge — and I don't even know what my edge is — or if something changes in the economy and I can't shift with it ..." He took a deep breath. "If I don't perform, I would be out of there in no time. There's no room in my work, not a smidge, for someone who is not performing."

"That sucks," I astutely observed.

"Big time."

"What about your friends? The ones from work?"

"There are two types of friends, Simon. The ones who are there when you are high-flying and the ones who are there when you are down in the gutter and need all the help you can get."

My father, the human being.

What can I offer up in return that would make him feel better? I wondered. And then it seemed obvious. I wondered if Andrea had put the lie in my head, made the suggestion. "Dad, about Ozzie. I wanted to believe he was real. But he wasn't, was he? I know that now."

My father smiled in a sad sort of way, and then he let out a big sigh as if a thousand-pound weight had just been lifted from his shoulders. The rain had let up, and it was not much more than a light drizzle.

I did a quick half glance towards the backseat and saw that Andrea was fast asleep again. I almost thought I could detect her snoring.

I was hoping we could make it home without stopping, but we needed gas. And I needed to pee badly. I slipped quietly out of the car and came back as quickly as I could. But much as I had feared, Andrea was no longer in the car.

CHAPTER FOURTEEN

I lied to my mother and told her we had a great time at the beach. My father corroborated my fib and held out his arm. "Do we look like we got a tan?"

"Maybe a little," my mom said.

No one said a word about Ozzie. Despite what I had said out loud, I had not given up on my old friend. Somewhere in my room, I was sure I had some hard piece of evidence to prove that Ozzie was as real as anyone. But I would not argue this with my parents. Maybe they thought they were trying to protect me from something, as they had so often before. Maybe something horrible had happened to Ozzie after he moved away and they didn't want me to know. Maybe my father had somehow fixed it today so my search had been in vain. I desperately wanted to know the truth. But maybe I wasn't ready for it.

"I'm thinking that I need a new car," my mother piped in, directing her announcement towards me for some reason. "I need it for my work. Can't be taking my clients around in an old beat-up rattletrap like what I'm driving."

Her "old beat-up rattletrap" was a two-year-old Mustang that had every accessory imaginable: super CD stereo system, power everything, mag wheels, sun roof.

My father didn't seem surprised. But he wasn't giving her one of his usual looks that said, *Oh boy, here she goes again. Nothing is ever good enough.* Instead, he was smiling and looking at me for some reaction.

My mom was still looking at me. "And Simon, you're seventeen now. Soon you'll have your licence and need your own car. So I was thinking that you can have the Mustang and I'll move up to something a tad more appropriate for my work."

I had always thought my mom was so attached to her Mustang that she'd want to be buried in it when she died. It had been one of her proudest possessions, what she called a "gift to herself" after three big commissions on some of the best real estate in town. Why she thought giving it to her lunatic son was a good idea I can't imagine, but I wasn't about to complain. The rules to the universe seemed to keep changing. Had I often wished for the Mustang as my own? Of course.

But I had wished for many things, and few had come true.

"But you have to keep taking your meds," she said.

Even in the new universe, there were deals to be made. "Of course, Mom," I said.

In a week or ten days, my latest supply (which had been flushed) would be supposedly consumed and I would receive a fresh supply of those shiny pills my folks paid so handsomely for. And, I supposed, I might have to begin taking them again. In the cock-eyed world of these two screwy adults, they sure as heck didn't want their son behind the wheel of a car unless he was taking drugs.

In my room, I thought much about Andrea and about Ozzie. I looked for a scrapbook that I remembered I had stashed away — maybe that had some photos of Oz and me. But in my scrapbook I could find none. There were some empty spaces where I must have removed some shots. And there were pictures of me with my new bike or a skateboard, but Ozzie wasn't there in a single scene. I even found one where I was wearing a safety helmet and knee pads (to please my parents, of course). The photo was ripped on one side as if someone had removed half of it — the side where Ozzie had been standing.

But I had the letters. I read them over again, studied the handwriting. I grew skeptical and took out some old samples of my schoolwork from those days. Essays I'd written on poltergeists and doppelgangers. Ozzie had this crisp, clear, printed handwriting as if each letter had been crafted with scientific precision. My own penmanship, at best, was a scrawl.

I reread my own work reflecting my lifelong interest in the unlikely occurrences of the past.

Between 1829 and 1845, a beautiful young teacher in France named Emily Sage was fired from sixteen different jobs because she had the habit of appearing two places at once. This scared her students a bit too often for her employers to accept. On one occasion she would be picking flowers with her students by the schoolyard and at the same moment appear to other girls to be sitting at her desk back in the classroom. The girls inside said they could touch the second Emily and that she seemed very real. Emily had no explanation for this ability except that she did say she was worried about the girls left inside "getting into mischief," so that must have prompted her double.

Lewis Spense defines these doubles as "the etheric counterpart of the physical body, which ... may temporarily move about in space."

I really liked using words with as many syllables as possible, a habit my teacher had been trying to break me of. I only received a B- on the essay because she thought I had not really done the research but instead had made much of it up. When I tried to show her the books I had used, she dismissed them as "rubbish."

My other essay, one of my old favourites, was about the Amherst, Nova Scotia, poltergeist. In part, it read thus:

Esther Cox lived in a big old house and odd things started happening after her boyfriend tried (and failed) to have sex with her. Soon afterward, odd noises started happening in her room. When others in her family went to see what was going on, Esther inflated like a balloon and rose up into the air.

An invisible hand scratched a death threat against Esther into the plaster of the wall, saying, "Esther Cox, you are mine to kill." In the days that followed, there were classic poltergeist activities. Knives flew through the air and stabbed poor Esther in the back. Fires broke out and Esther was charged with arson. When she was put in jail, the inexplicable activities stopped.

I had received a solid B on that one, perhaps because I had included my own youthful cockamamie explanation for the poltergeist activities. My conclusion read, "Thus one sees the complexity of the feminine psyche and how traumatic events might trigger unseen forces heretofore dormant in the environment." *Heretofore* was a word I had learned from reading old books on angels and miracles, so it found its way into my writings whenever I could plug it in.

It's curious that my parents were still such believers in prescription drugs as a path back to normalcy for me. They had not always received good advice from doctors concerning medication. While my mom was pregnant with me, she made the mistake of taking two different medications prescribed by two different doctors. The gynecologist gave her one thing for the nausea and her family doctor gave her another prescription for the backache. Even though I was not a particularly hefty baby, I apparently wreaked havoc with my mother's spine.

She continued on both drugs through many months of her pregnancy so she could continue to show houses to home seekers wanting to move up in the world. I was in my blissful cocoon kicking and elbowing my mother's gut every now and then at the most inconvenient moments and receiving, along with my daily sustenance, a never-ending cocktail of whatever was in the pink pill and the blue pill.

Once out of the womb, I burbled and blubbered, pooped in my pants, and vomited with great abandon, and, if the photos do not lie, I was a happy, slobbering infant with a slightly goofy look in my eyes and not a care in the world. But, by the time I was one and a half, the family doctor acknowledged my parents' fears that I was somehow different. No name was ever nailed down as to what my condition was, but the family doctor learned that while pregnant my mother had taken not only drug A but also drug B. And he said that was ill-advised. If he had known, he would never have let her continue.

"What should we do now?" I imagine my parents asking him.

"Raise him as if he is perfectly normal."

All things considered, they didn't do a bad job. My accident jumbled up the transmission lines between the before and after of my life at age twelve. So my memory is sometimes a big fragmentary jumble — that jigsaw puzzle with pieces still scattered around the room.

I think that my parents had almost split up at least a dozen times, although it could have been more than that. I have a feeling that my father, when he learned about my mother's error in mixing drugs, blamed her for my "problems" because I saw remnants of that blame lingering on into the arguments down through the years. When stuff goes wrong, adults have a bad habit of looking for someone to blame, as if that makes the problem better. It rarely does.

I didn't necessarily see my oddness as a "problem." For the most part, I liked myself and I liked the fact I was different. Lydia would, of course, confirm that many of my unusual traits were, in fact, positive ones. They were related to my future role of being a so-called healer. In a previous time or place, I might have been viewed as an exceptional person instead of a bit of a freak. Anyway, I figured I really didn't have any say in the hand of cards I was dealt, to use an old television cliché. And I was okay with that, too. I never remember feeling lonely as a child. I had the great skill of always occupying myself, or at least my mind, with something.

Such an inquiring mind is led to the usual dangers of matches, stoves, dogs that bite, attractive bottles of poisons, household cleaners, and the like. It also led me to knock a hole in a hallway wall with a large hammer to see where the voices were coming from. And I am sure that someone or something was luring me to walk out into traffic now and then or climb a very high tree or wander as far as I could from my parents, who were trying to buy new shoes in the mall store.

I checked my email to get my mind off the past. It was the usual waste of time: sex spam, hype for garbage I didn't want, junk mail from losers and creeps. One quick cryptic note from Lydia, however.

> Simon,
> Time is no longer your ally. You are two steps forward and one back. This is not about you. If you are the knight, you must move two steps forward and then over one space. That fourth woman in your life, and you know who she is, Montague says she is losing much of her energy. She will not be with you much longer. If I knew what you should do, I would say so. But I do not. Montague

says this, although I don't know what it
means: "Continue your research."
Lydia

The only research I had been up to lately was my
own navel gazing and my efforts to find Ozzie, but
maybe that was the wrong direction. What was the right
direction?

I received a bleep that I had one new item of mail.
It was from an address I did not recognize. And then a
single word appeared on my computer screen: "West."

I looked out my window at the sun setting in that
direction. Above, however, was that dark, brooding,
almost leaden sky we had seen over us on the beach.
But there on the horizon to the west was a thin line of
clear sky and the sun had burst through, painting the
entire outdoors in a magnificent coppery light. It was
just such a sight as this that had lured me in younger
years to climb out my dormer window and sit on the
roof and stay there until the stars came out, or until my
parents discovered me and my frantic father went running for the ladder stored in the garage.

CHAPTER FIFTEEN

My parents played their little game well, right up until Wednesday. On Monday and Tuesday they had both been home by five-thirty and we'd sat down to a quiet evening meal. We were all so nice to each other that I should have sniffed out the fact that it was too good to be true.

On Wednesday afternoon, my mom came home early. She was sitting at the kitchen table drinking a cup of coffee. "Simon," she said, out of the blue. "Your father has moved out after all."

"What?" I was floored.

My mother looked at the refrigerator, not at me. "We came to the conclusion that the timing was good. You are doing okay. We're all doing okay. Better to have the separation when we're not in the middle of problems and conflicts. He and I need some distance from each other."

"Have either of you thought about joining the space program?" I snapped.

"He says that he enjoyed spending the day with you Saturday and that he'll come pick you up next weekend and you two can drive back to the beach if you like."

"Great," I said sarcastically.

"Simon. Your father and I have known we were not meant to be together. We've known this for a long while, but we were waiting for a time when you were ready for it. When you were strong. And now's that time. You are doing really well."

There wasn't anything that I could say that would not be cruel so I went to my room. A room, especially your own bedroom, has a habit of changing the way it looks according to your mood. Sometimes my room looked liked a warm, private sanctuary away from the troubles of the world. Sometimes it looked like a happy, goofy, friendly place full of all the junk I'd accumulated as a kid. Today it looked like a dungeon.

Even with all the lights on, it was dark. The pile of newspapers and magazines still sat by the door, slightly taller now as the evidence of daily catastrophe, war, pain, and suffering grew.

At first, my mind fixed on the great irony of it all. While things had been bad, when conflict raged at home, my parents stayed together. Once we hit some seemingly smooth sailing, he moved out. Since we had become somewhat of a happy family, both parents agreed that now was the time to give up. I believed that, now that this step had finally been taken, now that I was "strong" enough to handle it, they would eventually divorce. There would be lawyers, and I knew that lawyers would bring out the worst in both of them. Once they became competitive as to who would get what, they would get greedy and it would get ugly. At that moment I was so angry with them that I wanted desperately to do something that would truly hurt them. But I let that thought pass.

The anger subsided and was quickly replaced by gloom. I lay down on my bed, and it felt like the strength had gone out of my body. I closed my eyes and drifted, let it overwhelm me. I'd been here before. I knew this feeling of sliding down an inclined tunnel into the earth. I was allowing myself to descend, and I knew that the further I slid, the harder it would be to come back up. But I didn't care.

The great safe refuge of the truly depressed is sleep. It found me easily that afternoon, and there were no dreams.

When I woke, it was early evening. I heard the television on downstairs. My mother was watching the news. I looked outside. One car in the driveway, not two. In the oak tree outside my bedroom window, three ravens were perched. They were looking right at me with those dark, inquiring eyes as if they were there waiting for me to wake up, waiting to tell me something. I opened the window and they flew away.

I thought about climbing out onto the roof as I had done as a child and just sitting there. I would wait for the stars to come out and maybe, if I stared long enough, I'd see something interesting. But I knew my father would not find me this time. He would not go running to the garage for a ladder to bring me down.

I took a deep breath, trying to ward off that all-too-familiar darkness again creeping up already in the back of my brain. If I were to give in to it again and again, I knew I was going to be in trouble. So I forced myself to do something, anything, to occupy myself. I started to turn on my computer to log onto a chess site and find an opponent but changed my mind and clicked it off while it was booting up.

Then I sat down at my desk and lifted the pile of newspapers from the floor. Not one UFO story. No new underwater archaeological discoveries of Atlantis. No news about cults in communication with aliens. Nothing but politics and the daily dirge of violence and crime.

But then there was this.

Ridgefield Girl Still in Coma

A teenage girl continues on life-support in the Ridgefield Hospital several months after accidentally taking an overdose of prescription drugs. Although in a coma, doctors are at a loss to understand the periodic bursts of brain activity. Gail Connolly, the girl's mother, says they are praying for their daughter every day and they believe she will recover. The Connollys' daughter, Trina, was, at the time of her accident, a popular, outgoing girl at Ridgefield High School and a member of the school's chess team.

Her parents have been unable to explain the girl's overdose and insist it was an accident. Hospital doctors suggest that, after such a lengthy period of unconsciousness, the longer someone is in a coma, the more difficult it becomes for the patient to recover. They do, however, find the situation has a glimmer of hope in that Trina's unusual brain activity is a sign that recovery may yet be possible.

There was a photograph of the two parents but none of the girl. I began to wonder about what her story was. Ridgefield was a suburban town much like my own. I knew some kids who went to Ridgefield High. In fact, we had driven by the school and the hospital on the way home from the beach. I wondered exactly how someone could "accidentally" overdose so massively on whatever it was that she took. Something told me there was a story behind her coma. Another unhappy family, another unhappy kid.

I knew that someone in a coma was totally out of it. It was a deep form of unconsciousness often leading to death. It was in some ways a kind of protective state that prevented a person with a life-threatening injury from experiencing pain.

After my own accident, I myself had been in a coma for nearly twenty-four hours. I had "gone" someplace else, and it had not been unpleasant. The hard part was coming back to consciousness and the pain that went with it. And then the confusion, the lack of connections.

I wanted to know what this Trina looked like and I went thumbing back through earlier newspapers but could find only two other small stories about the girl, Trina Connolly, about her accidental overdose. I was wondering about "where" she had gone to and if she would return. I was deeply curious about her and felt so terribly sad that a girl my own age was in such a desperate state. I reread the three short articles, and it began to sink in. The parents were praying and expressing optimism, but the doctors, without coming out and saying it directly, were indicating that it was unlikely she would recover. Too much time had elapsed. In that most recent story, from yesterday's paper, the one I had read first, the doctors sounded much less optimistic. Probably there was very little hope at all of her recovering.

I began to shake first and then I cried again. I cried for this poor girl, Trina, but I was also crying for me and I was crying for the whole sorry state of the world.

When I fell asleep, I started to dream. In my dream I was at the bottom of a very deep well. Fortunately (although the word seems ironic) for me there was no water in the bottom of the well. I had a very small flashlight in my hand, a key chain flashlight actually, the kind my mother keeps in her purse. I flicked it on and immediately realized the light's tiny battery was failing. It would soon be dead. It was attached to a set of keys, but they were not car keys. Instead, they were old-style skeleton keys like something from a very old house or maybe even a castle.

In my first flicker of dim light, I saw the walls of the well — smooth, wet stones, mossy. In the darkness, I realized that I could see the stars up in the night sky, the constellation Cassiopeia directly above me. Had I paid better attention in that History of Civilization class, I might have known something about the being the constellation was named for. But my mind had wandered often.

Was I frightened down there in this well of despair? Oddly enough, it was not as bad as how I had felt while I was awake and learning of my parent's separation. If I had been the cause of family conflict, I had also been the glue — the Crazy Glue to be precise. But the epoxy of me had failed. I wasn't cohesive enough. My family, as I had loved it and sometimes loathed it, was no more as far as I was concerned.

Which explains why my ever-fertile and entertaining subconscious mind put me in this well. A skilled lucid dreamer can make things happen in a dream. My astral projection skills had been coming along nicely, but I was a poor lucid dreamer. I willed all manner of interesting things to appear in dreams and they just didn't materialize. But I kept trying. I yelled out to my parents for help.

My voice echoed up through this deep chamber and spilled out into the empty night. Nothing. Maybe I would have been wiser to yell for Tanya or Andrea or even Ozzie. The Ozerater would never leave me stranded in a well. He'd at least toss me down a sandwich.

The quality of the silence reminded me of what it sounds like to be wearing some truly expensive stereo earphones with the stereo turned off. You feel removed from the world.

And so I had fallen into the earth, into this well or this chasm in the earth's crust. I was not on my way to hell but trapped part of the way there.

Then I heard breathing. Easy explanation: my own. It was echoing off the walls. I was always a heavy breather. A snoremeister in my sleep. In the daytime, I kept my mouth open, because my nose could never retrieve enough air to satisfy my demanding lungs.

Focus, I commanded my sleeping self. *Breathe in, breathe out. Stay calm. It is only a dream. We repeat, this is only a dream.*

The voice, I assumed, was the usual voice in my head, but I was sure the breathing now was coming from somewhere else directly behind me. I had been saving what was left of the depleted battery in the keychain light for an emergency, and this seemed as good a time as any. I flicked it on and turned myself around.

And there I was. Smiling.

Old Roger Sperry, the Caltech researcher who studied epilepsy patients whose connective right/left hemisphere tissue had been severed, drew some odd conclusions from his research. In essence, he had concluded that the "you" who you identified with most existed in the left hemisphere. There was somebody else holding down the fort in the right side of your brain. As a result some patients heard "voices in their heads." Well, doesn't everybody? Duh.

These patients were not like people with dual identity or multi-personalities or any of that sort of thing. They just had an amplified sense of what most people experienced. In the old days, that voice in your head may have been called a "conscience." Or some could have thought it was God.

Julian Jaynes, that other expert on brain activity, had concluded that our primitive ancestors were incapable of having this internal debate of trying to sort out what is real and what is imagined. As we evolved, we learned to sort things into two distinct categories of internal (imagined) and external (real world). We also began to have "conversations in our heads." We had discussions, arguments, parliamentary debates, polemical altercations, and ultimately intellectual and moral mud-wrestling going on up there. Or at least I did.

But I had never met my other self face to face.

He was rather calm and composed in the failing flashlight. For a right-brain creation, he seemed to have a handle on a very physical problem that involved problem solving.

The light went dead, and he spoke my name in a voice like the voice you hear when you first tape-record yourself. *That doesn't sound like me*, you say. But that is probably what you really sound like outside your own head.

Did I still think I was dreaming? I believe so. It was all a little surreal. Scary and interesting at the same time. (Like the first time I watched *The Matrix*.) The me who was not smiling, however, was considering when this dream was going to end. We were still in the damn well, and usually in a dream you flit about from one place to another. That same me was becoming fearful that I might not ever leave this strange place. I didn't want to stay at the bottom of a freaking well for the rest of my life, and I didn't know if my parents knew the right doctors who could throw down a rope.

My other self said it this way. "Simon, we have a problem here and basically only one solution. Where would you like to go?"

My left-brain me, ever so logical, suggested, "Up."

"Good. So we need a creative solution."

"I was hoping that's where you'd come in."

"You trust me then?"

"I've always trusted you," I said.

"Okay," my twin said. "The rocks are too slippery to climb, but if we lean into each other, back to back, and brace our feet against opposite walls, we can do it."

It seemed like a crackpot idea. "Can't I just will myself to wake?"

"It doesn't work that way," he said.

And so, back to back, Siamese twinned, with the hamstrings of our legs tight and straining against the wall, we ascended towards the waiting arms of Queen Cassiopeia.

CHAPTER SIXTEEN

I woke up with a sore back and a charley horse cramp in my leg, not knowing if I had reached the surface. I wasn't even totally sure if the vivid well of my dreams had been on planet earth.

My dream had prompted only one immediate decision. I would not go to school today. My mom was already off to the front lines of the real estate wars when the phone started to ring. I could see from the call minder it was my father calling from his office. I did not want to have that conversation. So I let it ring. He could leave a message. I had detected over the years, as the tensions mounted between us all, that we communicated better with each other by leaving messages on various machines and services. I think we could have held the family together if there was always a buffer of technology between us. It usually just involved stating the basics: who, what, where, and when. And we would leave out how and why.

Lydia had told me once that I was destined to do great things in the line of "communications." She interpreted this to mean that I could be an anchor man on a TV news show, a diplomat who could stop wars between warring nations, possibly even the first human to communicate with aliens already living undetected amongst us. Or maybe I'd just be a guy who hooked up cable to your house so you could get all the sports channels.

Back here on earth I was never a great conversationalist. As Lydia would say, it wasn't my "time" yet.

Alone in the kitchen drinking a cup of instant coffee (three sugars, lots of milk) I thought I might just spend the day reading the backs of cereal boxes. I was that motivated. But the newspaper was sitting on the table. In it was absolutely nothing of a metaphysical or occult nature, indicating to me that the whole day would be a great disappointment. I could see the forests of gloom already growing in the hallways, the vines of foul thoughts lacing up through the floorboards.

The newspaper reminded me of the unconscious Trina, a girl I did not know and had never met. I thought we had something in common. Boy in a well, girl in a coma. At the very least I wanted to find out what she looked like.

Riding a public bus involves being stared at. The eyes pinned me with various labels. *Dope addict. Runaway. Purse snatcher. Car thief. Pervert. Generic deviant.* You didn't have to be telepathic on a bus to know who thought what about you.

Fortunately for me, I was only going to Ridgefield, a mere twenty-minute ride west on Highway 17. I got off near the Wal-Mart and walked to the public library. The woman behind the desk there saw me coming and immediately sized me up as a hormone-crazed youth who wanted to use the public Internet access for pornography. She was surprised when I asked her if there was a collection of Ridgefield High yearbooks in the library.

"Over near the fire extinguisher," she said and pointed. I sat down beneath a portrait of Queen Elizabeth side by side with one of the presidents of the United States, an odd combo placed there as if the two were married. If so, I would have guessed it was an unsatisfactory union from the look on the queen's face. The president, meanwhile, had that familiar glazed-over look suggesting he was there but not there, as if his real thoughts were on a favoured golf game from a decade earlier, or maybe it was a look that said, "My mind has been taken over by the grey, almond-eyed ones from Tau Ceti."

I found last year's edition of Ridgefield High's oddly named yearbook. *The Shield* had a Roman shield on the cover and the motto "Prepared and vigilant" embossed in vinyl. Inside were all those smiling faces as if the photographer had waved a magic wand and made the students stupidly happy, as if the entire student body was this one gigantic mob of blissful teenagers headed on the bright yellow brick road towards beatific adulthood. It occurred to me that there are many kinds of lies in the world and a school yearbook is one of them.

I was not prepared for what was to be revealed to me as I turned the pages heading towards Trina's picture. The yearbook was a monument to alphabetical arrangement and the As the Bs had no surprises — pimply-faced boys and girls with last year's hairstyles. And every student was listed with his or her first, middle, and last names. That is often not a kind manoeuvre on the part of the yearbook committee, or it was perpetrated as a joke, since some of us go through life trying to ignore the fact we have middle names. Mine is Archibald, a memento to my father's grandfather, who was a miserly man who beat his son, my grandfather, until young grandpop ran away to work in lumber camp. I could hear the litany of three-part names being read at the future high school graduation by a cheerless principal, satisfied that another crop of youthful minds were about to move on. But I was not at all prepared for what I would find in the Cs.

I found her. She too was smiling. Trina Connolly. Or, as the book revealed, Trina Andrea Connolly.

With my finger holding the page, I closed the book and took a deep breath. I felt my heart race. The librarian was staring at me. I counted to ten and opened the book again. *Trina Andrea Connolly*. She looked younger, but it was unmistakably her.

I dreaded the thought of entering a hospital. My memories of my own hospital days were not my fondest. How much could I trust my own instincts on this? In some ways, it seemed clear that I was *supposed* to go to her. But maybe it was already too late. Maybe she was too far gone. So many weeks unconscious and possibly her parents were at the point of letting her go, pulling the plug on life support. Or was *that* part of why Andrea had revealed herself to me? Was I supposed to be the one to release her?

I made the mistake of entering the hospital by way of the emergency entrance and I walked in just as five car accident victims were being rushed past me. A child was screaming for her mother and blood was flowing out of her mouth. A woman, possibly the girl's mother, had a massive head wound and was unmoving, possibly dead. A man, conscious and bleeding over the eye, was strapped down and shouting something incomprehensible.

Everyone else sitting in the emergency room had a look of anguish on his or her face as this parade of human misery passed. Everyone except for a boy of eleven or twelve who sat alone, smiling. I remembered that boy's face so clearly. It was Ozzie. The Ozzie I had known. I took two steps towards him but stopped. He saw me and stared intently, stopped smiling. I was thinking that I must be mistaken. This was not Ozzie, could not be. He began to say something. At least his lips moved, and I thought he was saying my name, but I could not hear him. I would go no closer. I turned and walked away.

The one person I was certain I could not trust to be cool on this mission was the boy walking nervously through the hospital trying to discover the location of Andrea/Trina. Whenever I passed nurses or doctors, however, I pretended to be walking purposefully.

By the elevator, I found an extremely helpful diagram of the entire building. Third floor: Intensive Care, ICU. A coma needed intensive care. The door opened and I stepped in. I pushed 3. Two doctors had charts in their hands just like on TV but they were talking about basketball, about who would win a game tonight in Seattle.

I stepped out of the elevator into the hallway and discovered I was where I wanted to be. ICU. A quick flashback of my own hospital experience didn't help. It was the smell of disinfectant in the air, the cold buzzing of fluorescent lights, the sound of hard-soled shoes on the linoleum floors. It triggered an interior shouting match between logic and intuition. Logic told me to take a deep breath, decide this was not something I should be involved in, not anything I could handle.

Intuition (if that was the other debater) kept my feet moving forward. Right brain wins. There were ten rooms. Most had open doors. I didn't want to appear to be searching or lost or in any way conspicuous. I chose door number eight. A woman, a very old woman with tubes up her nose, lay there with eyes wide open staring straight at me as if she were expecting me. Her eyes were a piercing blue and she had great blue veins prominent on her forehead. She had only a few threads of grey-silver hair and the bones of her skull seemed ready to split open the pale skin.

Looking straight at me she held up one hand and crooked a finger. I somehow decided that what she was doing was pointing, pointing to the next room. I nodded.

I moved quickly to the neighbouring room, number six. The sound of beeping monitors. A curtain around the bed. I walked into the room and then entered the closed private space inside the curtained sanctuary.

A girl lying on her back. Motionless. A plastic mask fitted over her mouth and nose. A machine by the bed allowing her, or forcing her, to breathe. Pale skin. Eyes closed. Logic must have taken the stairs instead of the elevator and just then caught up with me here, telling me clearly and loudly: *This is not her.*

But I did not leave.

I looked up at the ceiling to clear my thoughts then back at her. I was convinced this was not the Andrea who had appeared to me. Not the girl from the yearbook.

But what would all those months in a coma do to a person?

On the night table was a photograph: a family. Mother, father, son, daughter. Outside, standing by a blossoming apple tree. The girl in the photo was most certainly Andrea. Radiant, alive. The great photographic lie of a beautiful young woman about to have the happiest of lives.

Before me, a living corpse. And now I had an overwhelming stone of sadness in my chest. The well of despair seemed to be opening up in front of me again. To stay there one more minute would mean walking the rim of that pit as it begged me to fall in.

There were voices in the room now. Hushed tones of adults talking.

When the curtains were pulled back, Andrea's parents saw this boy they had never seen before leaning over their daughter, then flinching back with a shocked look on his face.

The father spoke first. "What are you doing here?"

I tried to speak but nothing came out. I tried to frame the words in the air in front of me.

"Who are you?" the mother asked, her voice quavering with accusation in the way she pronounced the first word.

"I came to see Andrea," I finally blurted out.

"Andrea?" She looked puzzled.

I nodded.

"No one calls her Andrea anymore."

"Trina," I said, correcting myself. "I came to see Trina. I'm a friend."

Her mother studied my face. "You still call her by her middle name, her childhood name. No one has called her Andrea for a long time. From the time she was small." It was a kind of a question, I suppose. She wanted to know why. Everyone else knew her as Trina.

"She liked it when I called her Andrea," I said.

"I'm sorry I startled you."

Andrea's father cleared his throat, dropping his guard. "It's just that, well, all of her other friends have stopped coming."

"They've given up," Andrea's mother said, dropping her head so she was looking at the floor.

"Why didn't you come to visit before this?" her father asked.

"I didn't know about her until I read the story in the paper."

"You're not from Ridgefield."

"No. I'm from Stockton. I'm Simon. Andrea ... Trina, was a friend of a friend."

"Oh, I see. Emily Littleton moved to Stockton."

"Right," I lied. "I was a friend of Emily's."

Logic again reminded me I should leave. It said I could come back at another time. At least then her parents would feel a little more comfortable with me when I returned.

Her mother was opening up the curtain that surrounded the bed. Then she opened the blinds on the window. "I think we should let her have more light," she said. But it was a cloudy day, brighter by far in the room than outside.

And then suddenly it felt incredibly crowded in the room. I found it hard to breathe and I didn't know why. I felt the presence of many, many others. No faces, no bodies, no voices. But I was aware of them. The people who had died in this room.

"Are you all right?" Andrea's father asked. He saw the look on my face.

"I need to go now," I said. I shuffled my feet towards the door, but the others in the room were assaulting me. Some seemed to be pleading for me to stay, others insisting I go. No distinct words, just the conflicting pushing and pulling that was going on inside. It made me slightly dizzy, but worse yet, I was afraid I was going to throw up.

"Are you sure you are all right?" her father asked again.

I nodded.

Whatever I thought I had set out to do, it was clear I had done nothing. I had found her. And she was dying. Possibly already beyond any medical means of recovery. So many months in a coma probably meant she was brain dead. According to the paper, if the machines were to be turned off, her body would not keep her alive. She would be dead within minutes.

I regretted having come here. I had solved the mystery of who Andrea was, but maybe I would have been better off not knowing. Now I would be burdened by what I knew. I could not help her and, as it turned out, she had been of no real help to me. It seemed to take forever to go down the stairs, walk out of the hospital, and make my feet find their way down the street.

I walked past the library, past the bus stop, and out of town until I came to the abandoned rail line, the hiking trail that would take me towards the river and east, back home.

CHAPTER SEVENTEEN

Taking a long hike home is always a good time to do some serious thinking. When you are young and being swept about in great stormy seas with rogue waves of emotion, you are not in control of yourself. I was beginning to understand that if I went back on the medication, these emotional responses, these great monster waves that overpowered me as they tried to pull me down and drown me, would subside.

It was stress, one of my many doctors had argued. "Stress is all it takes and the mind of a young man can react in extreme ways. Emotional roller coasters. Sleep disruption. Lack of concentration. Auditory or visual hallucinations."

It had been pointed out to me before by these level-headed, pill-pushing, over-educated, boring doctors that the various inexplicable things I saw and heard simply were not there. If I wanted to be normal, I would have to stick to the solution that science had to offer.

I decided that I would ask my mother to set an appointment for a check-up. Like a kid with crooked teeth going to an orthodontist on a regular basis to get his braces tightened, maybe I needed regular tune-ups for my head. The kid with uneven teeth would one day have them straight and perfect. And me? Maybe if I just followed the plan, I would end up with a straight life.

I stopped by the bend in the river where Andrea and I had once stopped before. It was there she appeared.

"You were there in the room, weren't you?" she said.

"Could you see me?"

"No, and I didn't even sense you were there until you became so frightened."

I wouldn't tell her what I was feeling. About the others, the ones who had died there. "Why didn't you tell me who you really were?"

"Trina, you mean. Well, when I was six, I decided I wanted to go by my middle name, Andrea. My parents went along with it for a while but insisted I go back to being called Trina. I don't know why, but it was something we fought over. So, with you, I at least could use the name I wanted."

"Why did you stop coming to see me?" I asked.

"You didn't need me anymore."

"So you just drop in and out of a person's life?"

"Sorry."

"Besides, my life sucks now. I'm back to where I was before I met you. Only now it's worse. And now that I know who you are — where you are — I want to be with you. But I'm not even sure I can go back there. To that room, I mean."

"Maybe that's not really me. It's just what's left of my body. Maybe I've already left that behind."

"Well, maybe that's the part that hurts me the most," I said, feeling angry now. "It's almost like you reeled me in like a fish on a hook. I took the bait, I got to know you, decided that I cared for you, and now you are just going to go away. For good."

"It wasn't supposed to turn out this way. You weren't supposed to find me in that hospital bed."

"Tell me what happened. How did you end up there?"

"No," she said and stared straight into the water.

I expected her to be gone. This time for good. I was pushing her to take me someplace she did not want to go.

The water flowed on. The sun split through the clouds but only for an instant, as if offering hope and then taking it away in a heartbeat. The trees leaned over the river, as if listening to it, or us, as if waiting for something to happen. Big, green, silent hardwood trees — patient, tolerant. Ready for the good weather and the bad. Oaks. Maples. Black locust. Ash trees.

"My parents decided to split up after all," I said. "They did it *because* they thought I was doing well. So they figured the time was right. It would be easier on me. Easier on us all. Some people look for the easy way out." It was meant to be a kind of accusation.

And it had its effect. I turned away from her. And when I looked back, she was gone. Again.

Lydia was obviously stoned when I arrived at her apartment. I didn't particularly like her when she was that way. Door open as usual. Anybody could walk in. Amazing, since she'd been busted once — simple possession. But she continued to smoke. Never tobacco, of course. She called tobacco the devil's toolbox for some reason. But she argued that marijuana was a spiritual herb, a sacred plant. *Ganja*.

Lydia was listening to a CD of Gregorian chanting. I had to ask her to turn it down. Her eyes were a little glazed. "It's all about living in the present," she said without a word of hello. "The past is what imprints itself on you and makes it hard to move on to the next moment of time. If we could eliminate any memory of the past, I think we could live in the perfect present." The stoner's logic.

"If we couldn't remember the past, we wouldn't know who we were," I said. "We would be a new person at every minute."

"That's the beauty of it," she said. "No baggage. Total freedom. No ownership, no possession."

"Because you couldn't remember from one minute to the next whether that CD player was yours or somebody else's. Is this my house or my neighbour's?"

"Exactly. It would be wonderful."

"But it's not that way, and it will never be. We have to live with who we are, where we come from, what we've done."

She lost the hazy smile. "Point made. So, Simon. Give."

I explained about the queen I was trying to protect. Lydia grew more serious, collected the several leftover snubbed out ends of smoked joints, pinched them with her fingers, and, one by one, dropped them into a little film canister. "Always collect the roaches and keep them safe," she said, putting the lid on it. Then she shook the plastic film canister. "Never, ever throw away something you may need later." She touched her fingertips to her lips, then waved her hands over her amethyst crystal and rubbed her palms together.

She pulled her chair closer to where I sat. "Be still," she said. And she put her hands over top of my head, not touching, just allowing them to hover there. Next she closed her eyes, and a look of great concern came over her.

She opened her eyes and pulled back. "That's a lot of negativity you have there," she said. "A lot of potential there, too, but you'll have to get past whatever is holding you back. Let me see your hands."

It was like something my mother would have said when I was little, after I'd been outside playing in the mud with Ozzie or making some of our supposedly magical concoctions. "Let me see your hands," she'd say before a meal. And they would always be dirty, soiled with the creative artistry of being a curious kid.

But Lydia's intention was different. She held them one at a time in her own. She pressed with her thumb in the centre of both palms. Then she shook her hands in the air, "cleansed" them over her crystal, and ran her thumb down each of my fingers. She did her classic reaction: took a deep breath as if she had just discovered something.

"Focus on what you feel within you and do what your heart tells you to do. Don't look back."

I almost laughed out loud. This was *so* Lydia. Performing some little silly ritual then offering up something vague like this. Something positive and encouraging but oh so vague. I'd heard her say one of many variations of this line many times before to her paying customers and always they looked satisfied and happy with the decree.

"Now go," she said, smiling and rather pleased with herself.

The school had phoned. They always called to let my parents know if I was not attending. My mother wanted to know what was going on. So I lied and said I had had some bad headaches (my old stand-by) but that now I was better.

"Guess we both had headaches today," she said. "You wouldn't believe the people I had to deal with. They were all ready to buy the house. They'd been over every inch of it. And then they announced they found something better. Something perfect. So I wasted all that time."

"I'll go to school tomorrow," I said and walked off to my room.

It was back in History of Civilization class that Andrea returned. Mr. Holman was lecturing about the rivalry between the Athenians and the Spartans, a subject for which the entire class had no interest whatsoever. There was a lot of fighting in those days between the two and people died for reasons we found hard to comprehend today.

Andrea appeared here because she wanted to speak to me in a place where I could not respond. I was sitting in the back of the room by the window. I was staring out that window, trying not to think about Athens or Sparta. I was thinking about Andrea and then she was there, silhouetted by the bright light behind her.

"I've made my parents suffer long enough," she said, "and now I have to set them free."

I silently mouthed the word *no*.

"I had a lot of unhappiness in my life and now I'm ready to leave it behind. I'm sorry things didn't turn out better for you."

I could not let her make this decision. I raised my hand and asked for permission to leave the room.

Andrea followed me into the hallway. It was empty.

"Tell me what happened," I insisted. I touched her arm. I was squeezing it. She was very real.

"That hurts."

I was afraid that if I took my hand away, she would be gone so I held onto her. "Tell me how you ended up in that hospital bed."

She turned away.

I let go of my grip. "Please. I need to know."

She looked back at me and then down at the floor. "Like you, I was upset about my parents. They said awful things to each other. All the time. I hated being around them when they were arguing. But it had always been like that at home. When Craig came along, he made me feel different. He made me feel better about myself. I began to love my life instead of hate it."

"You fell for this guy, Craig?"

"Yes. I really did. He was a year older. I met him at

a dance. He'd had other girlfriends before, but for me, he was my first real relationship."

"But something happened."

"He was never cruel to me. He didn't want to hurt me. He was a great guy. He just lost interest. He said he was sorry. He said he knew it was a character flaw but he was like that. He couldn't help it. Craig would lose interest in one girl and move on. In this case, he lost interest in me and moved on to a girl named Cheryl. He said he wanted us to stay friends, though."

"And it made you feel terrible."

"I couldn't sleep. I couldn't function in school. I became very depressed. My mother took me to our doctor, and he prescribed an anti-depressant and sleeping pills. That night I swallowed them all."

"Was it really that bad?"

"You know, when you read about these things, when you hear about other people doing this, you always feel like there must have been another way for that individual. You always think that it can't be that bad, or that time will heal if you just give it a chance. Tomorrow will be another day. All that kind of crap. But it isn't like that."

Andrea was crying now. I didn't know what to do but stand there and listen to her.

"It isn't like that at all," she repeated. "All I could think about was trying to make the hurting stop. I wanted the pain to go away. And I wanted to punish my parents, I wanted to punish Craig, and I wanted to punish me."

I swallowed hard, not knowing what was the right thing to say. "And you did that. You punished everyone. I'm sure Craig felt it. I know your parents do. I saw their faces. But now you have to stop punishing them. Stop punishing yourself. I think you have to forgive them, forgive yourself, too."

She sighed. "That's why I'm leaving. They can't bring themselves to give the doctors the okay to end life support. I'm not sure the doctors can even do it. I could stay like that for months, years maybe."

"There must be some other way," I said.

"Simon, you better go back to class."

She started to walk away. "Don't go," I said. "Please don't leave me."

"I have to," she said and began to walk away down the hall.

I tried to follow, but my brain could not make my legs move. I was left standing alone in the hallway with a terrible feeling of cold swallowing up my body.

CHAPTER EIGHTEEN

I took the bus to Ridgefield, all the while sensing again that people were looking at me like I had committed a crime. My gut was tight, and there was an argument going on in my head. The two voices, one strong and confident, one pleading for me to leave everything alone, to go home and play chess against unknown adversaries on the Internet.

The first voice, the confident one, was the voice of a crazy person, urging me to act. *If you don't go through with this, you'll never be able to live with yourself. It's something you have to do.* I rubbed my hands together, and as I held out my index finger towards the seat in front of me, a charge of static electricity gave me a shock, a small thrill even. What was that about?

As I got up to get off in front of the hospital, walking down the bus aisle, I accidentally touched the shoulder of a man and the same thing happened. He jumped in his seat. It made me feel a little giddy. But it was just static electricity. That was all.

It was quiet in the hospital. Nurses and staff were moving about purposefully. I took the stairs instead of the elevator — maybe I didn't feel like being in a cramped space with strangers, maybe I didn't trust the technology today. Trying to stay focused on Andrea.

The door to her room was open, and I walked in. Both parents were there. Andrea's mother had been crying. Her father's face suggested he'd been wrestling inside with something very troubling.

"How is she?" I asked. "How is Andrea?"

"The same. At least we can't see any changes," she said.

"But the doctor says she's passing through a stage. A point of no return."

"It's been a long time. But I happen to know that Trina is strong," her father said.

"I'm a little surprised you came back. I know it's not easy being here. We appreciate it." Then he realized he was making me uncomfortable by saying that, reminding me how I had reacted before. He cleared his throat and tried to make small talk. "Did you, by any chance, ever know Craig? Was he a friend of yours?" her father asked.

"No," I said. "But I know who he is. Did he ever come to the hospital?"

"He came once," Andrea's mother said. "He brought flowers, but he didn't say much. He couldn't even look at her. I don't know why someone would bring flowers to an unconscious girl. Then he left and never came back."

"Trina took everything in her life so seriously." Her father was speaking of her in the past tense now, not a good sign. "She was always so ...," he fished for words from the air, "... so sensitive."

A word that had often been used for me. It is a condition of the mind and heart, I believe. Those like Andrea and myself, we feel things deeply. We sense there was more than what appears on the surface. When we aree happy, we soar. When things go wrong, we plummet.

I experienced this great nervous energy in my chest, the blood pounding in my ears. I understood that even now, Andrea's parents were feeling an intense guilt. As if this was their fault. Like Craig. He had felt it too when he saw her. That's why he couldn't bear to stay here.

"She was trying to punish you," I said out loud.

"What?" Her father was stunned.

"She was trying to punish you and Craig and the rest of the world."

"She said this to you?" her mother asked.

"Yes. It was the wrong thing to do. But it made sense to her."

"Simon, how long did you know her?" he said. "Trina never mentioned you. We never met you. You never came to the hospital until recently. Who exactly are you?"

I took a deep breath, considered telling the truth. At least my version of the truth — about how she had appeared to me in class one day. And how she came to help me with my problems. I almost blurted it out. My grandfather, now long gone, had once told me that sometimes, the only way out of the tough spot is to forget about consequences and just "spill the beans," tell the truth.

My grandfather, the world's most charming and kind man as far as I can remember, once "borrowed" money from a charitable organization he was volunteering for. He borrowed it to help a friend in trouble. The friend took the money, left town, and my grandfather was in a tight place. So he told the truth. And served three months in jail, lost his daytime job, and never did get back on his feet again. No, I would not tell the truth, after all.

"I wasn't aware that Andrea — Trina — was in the hospital until recently. I live in Stockton and hadn't really talked to her for quite a while. I had lost touch with her and wondered what was going on, but it wasn't until I saw your story in the newspaper that I came over."

Andrea's mother wiped her eyes with a tissue. "I think sometimes that maybe it was God's will that she be released. We love her so much, but maybe all of this is just unfair to her. The doctors don't think she can ever recover, that her mind will never be able to function properly. Sometimes I think we should let her go. For her sake."

I didn't know about God's will. I didn't know if I even believed in God. I could accept many notions of who we were and what we were. But I had not come to any conclusions about God. God was a big question mark in my life.

Andrea's father was angry at his wife now. They had probably had this discussion many times before. "It's not up to us to decide," he said.

"But what if all this is actually hurting her? We can't know what is happening to her, what she is experiencing."

Right then, I wanted to tell them the real story of me, of my accident, of what I had experienced while I was in a coma. But again, I knew that if I said too much, they would see how strange I really was. It wouldn't take much to scare them, and I needed their trust. I decided to tell them one true thing about me that might give them some hope. "I was in a coma once when I was young. And I recovered. Maybe she will too."

"But it's been so long," her mother said.

"Do you talk to her?" I asked.

"Yes," her mother said. "I sometimes think she can hear me and she can understand what I'm saying."

Her father let out a sigh as he spoke to his wife. "There is no visible reaction. It's what you *want* to believe."

"You don't speak to her?" I asked him.

He looked at his daughter. "I did for a while. But I don't anymore. I don't know what to say."

"How long have you been here with her today?" I asked.

"Three hours," he said.

"I'd like to sit with her for a bit, if that's okay with you. I'd like to speak to her, but I don't know if I can do it with you both in the room. It's something I was thinking about a lot. It may not matter if she can hear me or not. It's just something I need."

Her mother immediately nodded. Her father was not so sure, but he said, "We could use a break. Sure."

And so they quietly walked out and left me alone with Andrea in that devastatingly quiet hospital room.

I came close to Andrea — the hospital Andrea — for the first time. Her face revealed nothing. The monitors made predictable noises. An artificial breathing machine put air into her lungs in a regular rhythm. Her chest would rise and fall. But there was no other real sign that there was life in this body. I wondered if Andrea had already done as she said she would do. I feared that she had already "gone away."

I sat in the chair closest to her and closed my eyes. I had no plan. Nothing. I guess I expected she would help me. I thought she would appear — the other Andrea. But nothing happened.

I opened my eyes and began to speak to the girl lying in the bed. I told her my story. I told her everything about what kind of a kid I was, about my unusual qualities, my problems. I explained to her that I had spent my childhood so often alone, that my parents had tried to be good parents, but that I really was a big disappointment to them. I told her about Ozzie.

And I told her that I was now fairly certain that Ozzie had never existed. I probably had imagined him and made him so very real that I was willing to take advice from him and do any crazy thing he suggested. Crazy things that would come very close to getting me killed. But I told Andrea that I knew she was different. She had come to me for a reason. That's why I was here.

I touched her hand first, felt the lifeless quality of it, the coolness. I squeezed gently and I talked some more.

I told her that I could not explain to myself how a girl in a coma could have appeared to me. If it had not been for the discovery of her here, I would have soon concluded that she was another Ozzie, my next hallucination. No one, not even me, would deny that I had started out with problems, enhanced my problems with brain damage brought on by my accident.

I held both of Andrea's hands now and slid my hands onto her wrists, pressing them tightly. I could feel her pulse, the lifeblood still moving through her. I closed my eyes and had a sensation in my head of being weightless as if I was about to faint or in some way lose myself and drift. I let go.

When I opened my eyes, I saw small stars of a light all around the room, those tiny bright fireflies you see when you come close to passing out. My own heart was beating wildly with a great pounding in my chest.

In my head was a great stew of ideas and images. Medieval things. The laying on of hands. The curing of the sick by touch. Learning the truth of an illness by studying the lines on the palm of one's hands or feeling the energy points in someone's feet.

None of this was anything I had any true knowledge of. I was someone who dabbled in the realm of unlikely possibilities, that was all. Nothing more. I knew what this would look like if her parents returned or if a doctor came into the room. At the very least I would be forced to leave and never be allowed to return.

Holding onto her wrists, however, made me feel something that didn't feel right. I sensed resistance. She did not want me here. I opened my eyes and stood back.

Yes, I understood. She had already told me she would not reappear to me. The resistance I was feeling was understood. And very real.

But it convinced me that she knew I was here and she knew what I was trying to do. I think I understood why she was pushing me away. She was still trying to punish us all — me included now. If she died, she would complete what she set out to do: hurt Craig, hurt her parents, hurt everyone. Like me, Andrea had her own duality. She wanted to help and she wanted to hurt. One had become weak and the other stronger. She would die still wanting to hurt the people in her life.

And if she did, she would carry that with her to wherever she would go. Wherever her spirit went or her soul or whatever was left when we leave our body behind. And I could not let her do that. I realized then that I needed to change all that.

I let go of her arms and I placed one hand on her forehead. Now the sense of resistance was even more powerful. An insistence that I stop, that I leave her alone. At first, my own insistence to continue was creating a battle of wills. I was trying to overpower her. I was angry with her for wanting to do this thing to her parents and to me.

It was as if I could see this other Andrea in my mind now. I could hear her voice, insistent, edged with her own anger. *Leave me alone.* I could see that I needed to move past my own ego in this. I had to show her this was not a battle of wills.

I opened my eyes to discover that other Andrea standing in the room, as real as she had been at school. I moved away from the bed and towards her.

"I should have been gone by now," she said. "Staying here any longer just increases the pain. You don't know how badly it hurts."

"I can't let you do this. I want you to wake up."

"That's not fair. You should not be intruding like this. I'll prove to you why."

And at that instant I felt myself swept into a dark and terrible place without boundary and dimension, a hollow, hopeless realm of utter desolation. I felt diminished and experienced such loneliness and despair that it seemed those emotions were the entirety of my universe. And I realized this was how bad she had felt. Why she had wanted a way out. And then it faded.

I was still in the room with the girl in a coma. In a way, I was convinced by that brief experience of how terrible it can be for someone to hurt so badly that she wanted to end her life. And so I made what seemed to be the only decision that would make a difference.

I locked the door from the inside. I went to the wall and I pulled out the plugs on all the machines. The heart monitor did not have a chance to sound an alarm. The room was perfectly silent.

I stood beside Andrea's bed. Her chest was no longer rising and falling. I was convinced that if I touched her at all, she would in some way overpower me. So I stood there by the side of her bed and I simply said out loud, "I'm going to go with you."

I closed my eyes and felt myself swept into that darkness again. It was very real, very physical. It was not just the bottom of a well this time. I was in an overpowering vortex falling and spinning and losing all sense of control.

And then it stopped. I crashed down onto a cold, hard surface where the pain translated to another form. I had fallen onto the hospital floor and hit my head hard enough so that blood dripped from where I had split the skin.

I was breathing hard. Someone was knocking at the door. I couldn't focus, but I got to my knees. An old familiar headache, a piercing pain, was inside my skull. I grabbed the rail of the bed and pulled myself up, realized what I had done by unplugging the life support and felt a tremor of fear.

And I heard a human voice. A whimper, a cry, a kind of choking gasp. I saw her arm moving, almost waving as if she had no control of it. She was hitting at her face, at the mask on her face.

I steadied myself and looked at her eyes that so perfectly reflected the very fear I had just felt. As gently as I could, I pulled the mask from her. She coughed and spit something out as she gasped and cried out.

"It's okay. It's okay. It's okay," was all I could bring myself to say to her. And I put my hand on her forehead again, trying to calm her. But she let out a childlike, broken scream. I could tell from the look in her eyes that she did not know where she was. And she did not know who I was.

The resistance was still there. She was still pushing me away. But now it was different. Now I would leave her alone.

With my eyes still on hers, still hoping that she would show some sign that she remembered who I was, I edged away from the bed. To her I remained a total stranger who did not belong there.

I unlocked the door and it swung open. A doctor and a nurse burst in. The doctor looked straight at me, accusation in his eyes, but when Andrea cried out again, they both turned to her. "My God," the nurse said. "My God."

Shaken, and still filled with my own confusion as to what had just occurred, I gathered my strength and moved out of the room. Andrea's parents were walking down the hall towards me and were not aware of anything that had happened yet. As I approached them they could see that I was acting very strange. And they saw the blood on my forehead. I did not speak to them. I lurched forward, my head still pounding with pain. And I ran.

CHAPTER NINETEEN

Seventeen is an age that is both too young and too old. I think that if I were still, say, fourteen, I would have viewed the events differently. I would have said to myself, *You're still just a young, stupid kid. There are a million things you don't understand. This is just another one of them.*

My mother bought herself that new car. "I'm trying to reinvent myself," was the way she explained it. New car, new hairstyle, new clothes. She even had a new way of treating me. Well, sort of. She'd leave me notes on the table about what I should eat for breakfast and what we would have for dinner. But food for me was something I ate to keep myself going. I was a joyless eater at best.

The Mustang was mine, but I didn't have a driver's licence and I hadn't taken the driving course yet. I sat in it in the driveway, though. Quite a bit. I sat there alone, with the windows down, and I would think.

So seventeen was old enough to be sitting in your own car in your driveway sifting through the wreckage of your life. But it wasn't old enough to have a clue as to what it was all adding up to. I didn't know what anything meant. I kept hoping the events of recent weeks would make sense but it was all a big jumble.

Twice, well, maybe more than that, I had assembled all I knew about Ozzie and decided that my conclusion had been wrong. If I could keep searching, I would find the now seventeen-year-old Ozman somewhere, in some other town, egging on a friend, giving bad advice, and probably getting someone else into a lot of trouble.

But I didn't see any future in rooting around in the past, whether it was studying ancient civilizations like Sumeria and Babylonia or whether it was my own strange childhood days. I was purposefully trying to fail Mr. Holman's class, and I think he was going to pass me anyway, out of pity. Most people tend to frown on teachers who pass kids because they feel sorry for them, but I think it is an admirable trait. I think sometimes you just have to move on, and if you have a big whacking gap in your education — if you know next to nothing about Carthage or polynomials or Archduke Ferdinand — well, you'll probably just be able to get on with your life anyway.

I don't know why the cops would have bothered to bust Lydia again, but they did. Someone in her building must have thought she was an annoyance and probably told the police Lydia was growing marijuana and selling it. Sure, they found some of her weed. She never hid it, and you could always smell that sweet "herbal" smell in the hallway. She was fined and released.

"I should have seen it coming," Lydia said to me. "I'm in a vulnerable phase right now. Anything could happen. I'm going to lay low for a while and wait for my planets."

I wasn't exactly sure which planets she was waiting for, but I got the picture. "And what about your queen?" she asked, after I'd heard all about the rudeness of the police, the pettiness of the law, and the small-mindedness of a government that still had laws against an ancient, natural remedy for loss of appetite.

I told her about Andrea and about what happened in the hospital. She was wide-eyed. "Have you tried to talk to her since?"

"She doesn't know who I am. I went back to Ridgefield. I went to her house and waited until she was outside, just walking around looking at flowers in her yard. I walked up towards her on the sidewalk. And stopped. She looked up at me, said, 'Hi.' But I could tell that she didn't have a clue. She did not remember me at all. So I kept on walking."

"The Andrea who appeared to you may not be in full communication with the one who is now awake. It could stay like that for a long time. In fact, if she is still recovering, you shouldn't force it. It's possible she'll never remember."

"I know. That's what I was thinking. There was a story in the paper. The doctors said that sometimes, after a long coma, a chemical is triggered in the brain, the body's last-ditch effort to survive. It's rare. It releases a kind of shock treatment to the nervous system. They think that's what happened. They say she has memory problems, gaps, and some difficulty with language that should go away. Everyone is happy, though, and they don't particularly care how she was brought back."

"Didn't someone see you there at the time?"

"Her parents knew I was there. They knew that some strange teenager named Simon, a kid unfamiliar to them but claiming to be a friend, had been there. And then he disappeared. I didn't even get a mention in the paper. Maybe they assumed I had just accidentally been there when it happened. Maybe that's all there was to it."

"Simon, she's better. Why are you so sad?"

"Because I lost her. Because now all I have is me."

"What am I?" Lydia said, pretending to look a little hurt. "Am I nothing?"

"Sorry. I didn't mean that. It's just that the past looks better to me than what is ahead. I wake up in the morning and it takes all the energy I can muster just to get out of bed and stay awake for twelve hours."

"You have your whole life ahead of you," she said.

"Boy, that's original."

"Well, it's true."

"So this is what it's going to be like? No meteors crashing in the backyard, no aliens communicating to me from space, no wizards, no witches, no flying carpets, no telepathic ravens?"

Lydia had been infected by my sadness, and I now saw that she shared what I was feeling. Despite what I'd been through, or maybe because of it, I had triggered an inner realization that what had happened probably would never happen again. I felt like I was changed somehow. I was older, more reasonable even. Maybe I was becoming normal. It was a kind of death. The death of possibility.

And I didn't know if this sense of loss, this feeling of great sadness, would go away or if I would carry it around for the rest of my life.

CHAPTER TWENTY

A week went by, and I tried again to make contact with Andrea. I skipped out of my own classes early and waited for her outside her school, feeling a little like a stalker. I even got on her school bus and sat down beside her. "Andrea," I said, "I'm Simon. We've met before."

I guess it's the way I said it, the way I was acting. She was totally creeped out. She looked away from me at some other kids she knew on the bus. Her look was loud and clear. She didn't know who I was and she thought I was coming on to her in the most obvious and obnoxious way.

"Why are you calling me Andrea?" she asked, clearly annoyed.

"Um. It's your middle name, right? Didn't you once want everyone to call you that instead of Trina?"

"Oh, the yearbook thing. Is that it?"

"Yeah, that's it," I said. I guess I was hoping that something would click in her memory, that a light would go on and she would remember everything about me. I didn't know what to say next. Other kids on the bus were looking at me. The whole scene was feeling weirder by the minute. I could see the bus was coming to its first stop, and a couple of kids were getting up to leave.

"Well," I said, knowing this was probably the last time I would talk to her, "be good to yourself."

She gave me a quizzical look as I stood up. I reached out and almost touched her hand, but pulled back and went quickly to the front of the bus, tripping once on somebody's backpack that was in the aisle. Someone laughed. At the front, the door had closed, and I stood there for a second as the driver reopened it. Everyone on the bus was looking at me now. No one on the bus knew who I was.

I read in a book somewhere that the mind is a kind of immense dark castle with many, many rooms where most of them remain locked. If they were opened all at once, we would go insane. Sometimes, we open up an old, familiar, comfortable room and sometimes we open up a room where we've never been before. What is inside can be wonderful or terrifying. I was coming to the conclusion that I had lost my set of keys —

skeleton keys, no doubt — to many of those rooms in my dark castle.

I took my first hands-on driver's training class and nearly sideswiped a Pepsi truck and came close to flattening a pair of pedestrians who apparently could not read the "Student Driver" sign on the front of the car. It would take a while before I could become a competent driver, but I was on my way to all the freedom that driving meant to a young man. I now had a set of keys to a Mustang, and I cared less about those lost skeleton keys that might as well stay lost.

I also lost interest in my clipping files, even the orange one, so I moved the box into my closet. While avoiding doing homework one night, I reread a book Lydia had given to me for my birthday: Aldous Huxley's *Doors of Perception*. In it, he writes, "Each person is at each moment capable of remembering all that ever happened to him and perceive all that is happening everywhere in the universe. The function of the brain and nervous system is to protect us from being overwhelmed by this mass of largely useless and irrelevant knowledge ..."

If that was true, then the job of the mind was more to filter information out than to let it through into consciousness. And the end result is that the better you can do this, the more you become "normal" or mature or sensible or all of the above. And eventually someone, if you are lucky, hands you the keys to a Mustang, and you take a few driving lessons and drive off into the sunset.

My father skipped his first two weekend father-son outings because of two extremely urgent and important golf games with clients that he'd been trying to line up for a long while. He took me out for pizza, though, a couple of times and we went to see the latest *Matrix* sequel at the movies.

The next weekend, however, he did show up as promised and said we were driving to the beach. We'd stay overnight at a motel there. I expected that when we got there, we wouldn't do much of anything but maybe lie on the beach and run out of things to say to each other, then watch TV at the motel.

Instead, he was full of surprises. He was in a great mood, and he wanted to listen to my CDs on his new CD player the whole way there. After we'd checked in to the Flamingo Motel right on the beach, we walked down the boardwalk to a surf shop called Happy Dudes.

"I'm gonna rent you a board and buy you a surf lesson," my dad said as we stood before the shop.

I felt like I had been hit by a piece of lumber — but in a good way. An old, grizzly-faced, balding guy inside made me sign a paper that said we wouldn't sue if I was "maimed, injured or killed" while renting the gear. My father paid with his Visa card. The old guy tossed me a wetsuit. "Water's still cold enough to freeze your nuts, so you need this," he said.

We waited on the beach, me in my wetsuit, my dad just sitting there smiling up at the sun through his Rayban sunglasses. When the instructor arrived it was a blonde-haired guy in his early twenties. He looked a lot like the guy who had been in my dream in the hospital, my vision. I shook his hand, and he yanked me up onto my feet. "The first thing you have to remember about surfing is that the wave is a whole hell of a lot more powerful than you are. Respect that. Use that energy, tap into it, but don't fight it. You'll do okay."

I'd like to tell you I was an amazing surfer and that I picked right up on it the first day out, that it was righteous and I was a natural.

But it wasn't anything like that.

The waves were overhead. The water was cool — well, frigid is a better word. I got worked over seriously, dragged back to shore by waves several times before I could even make it past where the waves were breaking. My coach, who went only by the nickname Thumper, congratulated me when I finally paddled through the waves and made it "outside" to a place beyond the smashing waves where I could sit and get my breath back.

Thumper saw a set of waves approaching and told me to let the first four waves pass by. I watched as other surfers took off and slid gracefully down the face of the head-high waves. Wave number five was mine. As advised, I paddled like a madman, and I soon felt the wall of water swell up beneath me. I felt myself rising and then dropping, sliding down the cool blue wall of ocean. It was the most amazing thing I had ever known — the speed, the power, and the water. Everything moving.

But like every other first-time surfer, I think, I wasn't really prepared for what was going to happen next. The nose of my board plunged into the flat water at the bottom of the wave, driving the board and me down under. I took it face first, and the impact felt like the skin was being ripped off my face. And then I went under, holding my breath, the cold of the water shocking my system. When the crashing wave slammed down on top of me it seemed like I'd been hit by a bomb. Then I was twisted around like a pretzel, punched and pummelled and held under long enough to make me come to the conclusion I was about to drown.

At which time, my arms did a wild frantic dance and pulled me to the surface. The wave had passed. The sun was shining down on me and my board was only a few feet away. I dragged myself back up on it. The set of waves had passed. The water was now momentarily calm. I could see my own marbled reflection in it as my lungs gulped for air. But I did not feel bad. I felt great. I think there were several doors in that haunted castle of my brain opening and closing at once.

I saw Thumper sitting on his own board further out to sea, waving at me to paddle back out. "Good one, dude!" he shouted. He had a big grin on his face. With some difficulty, I figured out how to turn my board around and lie on it without falling off, and I began to paddle back out to sea. My heart was beating wildly in my chest and I was still gulping for air when a large grey and white seagull swooped down over my head, close enough to momentarily blot out the sun. He swooped low, and I felt the air compression from his wings as he rose back up into the sky. And the sound of the gull's voice was the unmistakable sound of laughter.

As I steadied myself on my board, I saw this kid walking down the beach, a tall, lanky, pale teenager with a great shock of hair that stood straight up. I squinted my eyes to get a better look. I couldn't help myself when I realized who it was. I yelled his name as loud as I could and waved frantically.

He stopped in his tracks and looked out to sea. I waved again and began to paddle towards shore as if my life depended on it.

PONY PALS

The Pony and the Lost Swan

Jeanne Betancourt

Illustrated by Paul Bachem

A
LITTLE APPLE
PAPERBACK

SCHOLASTIC INC.

New York   Toronto   London   Auckland   Sydney
Mexico City   New Delhi   Hong Kong   Buenos Aires

Thank you to Sue Holloway, PhD, author of *Swan in the Grail*, and to Hope Douglas, director of Wind Over Wings Wildlife Rehabilitation and Education Center, for sharing their knowledge and love of swans.

ISBN 0-439-30644-2

12 11 10 9 8 7 6 5 4 3 2 1   2 3 4 5 6 7/0

Printed in the U.S.A.   40
First Scholastic printing, March 2002

Contents

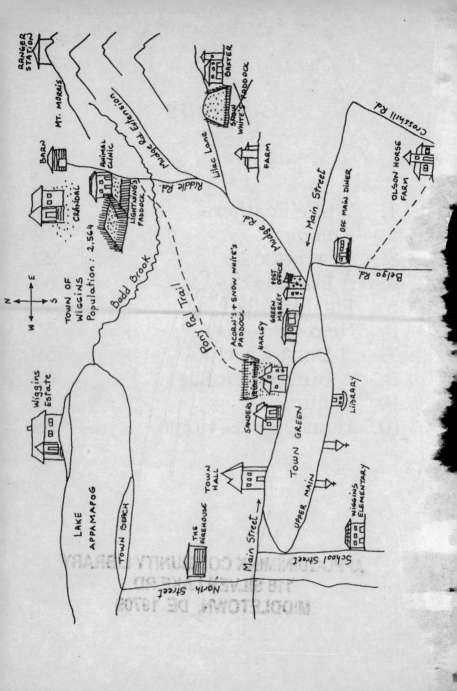

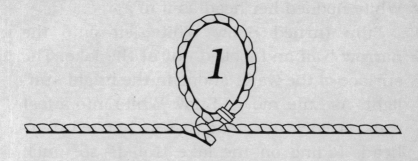

White Feathers

Lulu Sanders rode her pony, Snow White, along Badd Brook. Lulu and her friends were going for an afternoon trail ride around Lake Appamapog. Lulu halted Snow White at the beginning of the lake trail. Anna and Pam rode up beside her on their ponies, Acorn and Lightning.

"Let's ride to the beach," suggested Lulu.

"The ponies can wade," said Anna. "Acorn loves to do that."

Lulu patted Snow White's neck. "You like

1

to wade, too," she reminded her pony. Snow White nodded her head as if to agree.

Lulu turned Snow White left onto the narrow trail and looked out at the lake. The surface of the water shone in the bright sunlight. As Lulu moved Snow White into a fast walk, a flock of Canada geese honked overhead. Riding on the lake trail is so much fun, thought Lulu.

Suddenly, Snow White stopped and lowered her head to smell the ground. "No grazing," Lulu scolded as she gently pulled up on the reins. Snow White tugged against the reins and nickered. Lulu saw that Snow White wasn't trying to eat beach grass. She was sniffing a big white feather. There were more white feathers near it.

Pam and Anna halted their ponies. "Why'd we stop?" asked Pam.

"Snow White found some feathers," answered Lulu as she dismounted.

Anna and Pam slid off their ponies, too. The three girls studied the sandy strip of lakefront. They saw a lot of feathers. Some were big. Some were small. But they were all white.

Anna picked up a few feathers. "What kind of bird has feathers like these?" she asked.

"They look like swan feathers," answered Lulu.

The Pony Pals scanned the lake. But they didn't see any swans.

"We can't see the whole lake from here," observed Pam as she gathered a few feathers.

Anna stuck her little bouquet of feathers in the side of Acorn's halter. Lulu collected feathers for Snow White's halter, too.

"Let's look for swans," suggested Anna as she mounted Acorn. "I've never seen them in real life."

"I have," said Pam. "They're really beautiful and big."

"I saw a lot of swans in England with my father," said Lulu. Lulu loved the big white birds and knew a lot about them. She hoped there would be swans on Lake Appamapog.

The Pony Pals continued along a winding

trail toward the town beach. When the trail straightened out, the view opened up. Lulu halted Snow White and pointed to a white swan gliding gracefully along the water. Three baby swans followed.

Pam pulled Lightning up beside Snow White. "That's so beautiful," she whispered.

Snow White looked out at the swans and whinnied softly.

"The babies are adorable," added Anna. "But they're brown, not white."

"They'll turn white later," Lulu told them. She looked through her binoculars. "The babies are called cygnets. The swan with them is probably their mother. The females are smaller than the males."

"I wonder where the father is," said Pam.

"Maybe the mothers raise the babies alone," suggested Anna.

Lulu shook her head. "Swans mate for life," she explained. "The fathers help raise the cygnets."

"Let's stop here and watch them," suggested Pam.

"Okay," agreed Anna.

While the ponies waded and drank from the edge of the lake, the girls sat on a log to watch the swan and her babies.

The cygnets climbed onto their mother's back and slid back down.

"That is so cute," giggled Anna. "It's like their mother is a slide."

"Sometimes they hide under their mother's wings," commented Lulu.

The cygnets swam around their mother. After a few turns, they climbed up her side again. This time they stayed under her wings. A few minutes later, they slid back into the water.

Lulu loved the graceful way the mother moved her long neck. Her feathers glowed in the sunlight.

"*White Feathers*," Lulu whispered. "She's White Feathers."

"How do you know her name?" asked Pam.

"It just popped into my head," said Lulu.

"It's a perfect name for her," said Anna.

"Let's call her White Feathers," agreed Pam.

"Tell us more about swans, Lulu," added Anna.

"They like to hear people singing," remembered Lulu. "I sang a lullaby to the swans in England. Two of them moved their necks and wings to the music. It was like a dance."

"Let's sing to White Feathers and her babies," suggested Anna.

The girls sang, "Row, Row, Row Your Boat." First, they sang in unison. Then they sang it as a round.

White Feathers swam closer to shore. The cygnets followed.

Next, the Pony Pals sang, "Make New Friends but Keep the Old."

White Feathers faced them, balanced on her tail, and waved her wings.

"Wow!" exclaimed Anna.

"She's saying *hello*," explained Lulu.

The largest of the three cygnets tried to imitate his mother. He fluffed up his little wings, but they didn't fan out.

Lulu looked over at the ponies. Acorn and Lightning were ignoring the swans, but Snow White was watching everything they did. She nickered softly.

"Snow White likes them," observed Pam.

"Let's name the cygnets," suggested Anna.

"*Friendly* would be a good name for that big one," said Pam. "Because he tried to wave to us."

"Perfect," agreed Anna.

"What about the littlest one?" asked Pam.

White Feathers swam smoothly toward the middle of the lake. Lulu looked at the cygnets through her binoculars. Two of the cygnets stayed near her. But the littlest cygnet trailed behind. "Let's name her *Slow-poke*," she suggested.

"That's cute," agreed Anna. "I like it."

"Now what about the middle-size one?" asked Pam.

"You name her," said Lulu as she handed Pam the binoculars.

Pam looked through the binoculars. "Look," she said, "the middle-size one keeps putting her head in the water and her bottom sticks up."

"She's trying to eat from the lake," explained Lulu.

The cygnet bobbed back upright and tried to go under again. Her little bottom pointed to the sky.

The girls giggled.

"She's not big enough to do it right," explained Lulu. "She's practicing."

"*Bottom Up*," said Pam. "Should we call her Bottom Up?"

Anna and Lulu agreed that Bottom Up was a perfect name for the cygnet.

The Pony Pals watched the swans until they swam out of sight.

"Maybe we'll see White Feathers, Friendly, Slowpoke, and Bottom Up from the town beach," said Anna. "They're heading in that direction."

"I wish we'd see the father, too," said Lulu.

Anna took the lead and the Pony Pals continued along the trail toward the town beach.

"There's Mr. Kline," Anna called to her friends.

Lulu recognized the Klines' red pickup truck and saw Mr. Kline fishing from the shore. The Klines owned the local hardware store. The Pony Pals often baby-sat for five-year-old Mimi Kline and pony-sat for her mischievous pony, Tongo. The girls liked the Klines.

Mr. Kline saw the Pony Pals and waved. They waved back and rode over to him.

"How are the Pony Pals?" Mr. Kline asked.

"Great," answered Pam and Anna in unison.

"We saw swans," Anna told Mr. Kline as she dismounted.

"A mother and her three cygnets," added Lulu.

"I've seen them," said Mr. Kline. "They're beautiful, aren't they?"

"Yes," agreed Pam. "But there was no father."

Lulu and Pam slid off their ponies, too.

"Did you see a male swan?" asked Lulu.

Mr. Kline reeled in his fishing line. "Yes," he answered. "That swan couple came to the lake a couple of months ago."

Anna looked around. "I wonder where he is now," she said.

"The male was killed last week," Mr. Kline told the Pony Pals.

Anna gasped.

"That's so awful," said Pam in a hushed voice.

"How was he killed?" asked Lulu.

"He was shot with a bow and arrow," answered Mr. Kline. "His mate was very upset. I heard that she swam around the body for a long time."

No one said anything for a few seconds.

"We call the mother swan White Feathers," said Anna softly.

Lulu brushed her hand over the white feathers in Snow White's halter. Are these the dead swan's feathers? she wondered.

Enemies

The ponies drank from the lake while the Pony Pals talked to Mr. Kline about the swans.

"Why would somebody kill a swan?" Pam asked Mr. Kline.

"For sport," he answered. "Or to get rid of it. A lot of people think swans are fierce and dangerous."

"Are they?" asked Anna.

"Swans are big birds and very protective of their young," answered Mr. Kline. "So some people are afraid of them."

12

The three cygnets swam around their mother.

"There were four cygnets the last time I was here," continued Mr. Kline. "I guess one of them didn't make it."

"Poor little cygnet," said Anna sadly.

"White Feathers lost her mate *and* one of her babies," observed Pam.

"Was the cygnet shot with a bow and arrow, too?" asked Lulu.

"I don't think so," answered Mr. Kline. "I bet a snapping turtle got it. They go after cygnets and goslings. Or a hawk could have swooped down and taken it."

"The father wasn't there to help protect them," said Lulu.

"I hope nothing happens to the other babies," added Anna.

"There are a lot of dangers to wildlife in a lake," Mr. Kline told them.

"Like pesticides and trash," put in Lulu.

"Right," agreed Mr. Kline. He held out a length of fishing line. "And this stuff."

"Fishing line?" said Pam. "How is that dangerous?"

"People are careless about their fishing line," he explained. "When a fishhook gets caught on something, some fishermen cut the line off at the pole. That leaves tangles of fishing line in the water and in the bushes."

"Birds could get tangled up in it," commented Lulu.

"There must be hooks in the water, too," observed Anna.

"That's right," agreed Mr. Kline.

Lulu spotted White Feathers and her cygnets in the distance. She hoped they would stay safe.

Mr. Kline looked at his watch. "I better get on with my fishing," he said. "I have to be back at the store in an hour."

"We're going to the diner," Anna told him.

Anna's mother owned the Off-Main Diner, so the Pony Pals could eat there whenever they wanted.

"Your mother's diner is the best in Wiggins," said Mr. Kline with a wink.

"It's the only diner in Wiggins," giggled Anna.

14

The Pony Pals led their ponies out of the water. They mounted and said good-bye to Mr. Kline.

"If you girls find any fishing line, bring it to the hardware store," he said. "I recycle it."

"We will," agreed Pam.

The Pony Pals rode onto the lake trail and headed back toward Badd Brook. Whenever they had a view of the lake, they stopped and looked for the swans.

As they rode, Lulu thought about her Pony Pals. Pam and Anna loved the outdoors, wildlife, and ponies as much as she did.

Pam Crandal knew the most about ponies. Her father was a veterinarian and her mother was a riding teacher. Pam could ride a pony before she could walk. Lightning and Pam were an excellent jumping team.

Anna Harley learned everything she knew about ponies from Pam. They'd been riding together since they were in kindergarten. Anna didn't have her own pony until she was ten years old. Before that, she rode the ponies at Mrs. Crandal's riding school. She

15

also loved to draw and paint ponies. Because Anna was dyslexic, reading and writing were difficult for her. But she was an excellent artist. Anna's painting of Snow White was hanging in Lulu's bedroom.

Lulu knew more about wildlife than her friends. Her father was a naturalist who studied and wrote about wild animals. Lulu's mother died when Lulu was only a few years old. After that, Lulu traveled all over the world with her dad. But when she turned ten, her father decided that Lulu should live in one place for a while. That's when Lulu moved to Wiggins to live with her grandmother.

There aren't any elephants, giraffes, or kangaroos to study in Wiggins, thought Lulu. But there are plenty of other animals and birds to observe. Maybe I'll be a naturalist like my father when I grow up. Or will I be a detective?

Anna and Pam were always saying that Lulu was a great detective. Lulu believed that being a naturalist and a detective was part of being a Pony Pal.

"Hey, it's the Pony Pests," a boy's voice shouted from behind Lulu.

Lulu knew who it was without turning around. Tommy Rand and Mike Lacey. They were older boys who liked to tease the Pony Pals. Lulu thought the boys were immature and annoying. Sometimes Mike could be okay. But only when he wasn't with Tommy Rand.

"Should we outride them?" asked Pam. "We're faster."

"Yes," agreed Anna as she moved Acorn into a gallop. Lightning and Snow White picked up speed, too.

The boys' shouts became fainter.

Lulu slowed Snow White to a halt.

"Wait," she yelled to her friends.

Anna and Pam pulled their ponies up beside Snow White.

"I bet Tommy and Mike fish," said Lulu. "We should tell them about the problem with fishing lines at the lake."

"Good idea," said Pam as she halted Lightning.

17

The Pony Pals turned their ponies around to face the boys and block the trail.

Tommy screeched his bike to a halt. "Hey, get out of the way!" he shouted.

Acorn whinnied at Tommy.

Snow White backed up two steps. She didn't like bikes. Lulu thought she didn't like Tommy Rand, either.

"We have something important to tell you," Lulu told the boys. "About the lake."

"Do you fish?" asked Pam.

"What's it to you?" Tommy asked back.

Lulu took a deep breath. She wanted to gallop away from the boys and leave them in the dust. But she also wanted to protect the wildlife on the lake, especially the swan and her cygnets.

"Sometimes fishermen hurt birds and other animals around the lake," said Pam, "even though they don't mean to."

"How?" asked Mike.

"What do you care?" Tommy grumbled at Mike. "You're just catching fish."

Lulu ignored Tommy and told Mike what they learned from Mr. Kline.

"Let's go, Mike," Tommy said to Mike as he got back on his bike.

"Sure. We're out of here, buddy," agreed Mike as he hopped on his bike.

Lulu pulled Snow White out of the way.

The boys rode their bikes around the Pony Pals and continued on the trail.

"The BORING Pony Pests!" shouted Tommy over his shoulder.

"The DUMB, RUDE Bike Buddies!" Anna yelled after them. Acorn nickered in agreement.

"I hate how Mike does whatever Tommy wants," said Pam.

"He thinks Tommy is so great," said Anna. "But he's not."

"That's for sure," agreed Lulu as she and Snow White took the lead on the trail.

Half an hour later, the Pony Pals were in their favorite booth at the diner. They each had a grilled cheese-and-tomato sandwich and shared a big plate of french fries. Lulu pushed the fries in Pam's direction.

"If people like Tommy Rand are fishing on the lake," said Lulu, "White Feathers and her cygnets are in danger."

"What can we do to protect them?" asked Pam.

Lulu thought about White Feathers and her three cygnets. White Feathers didn't have a mate to help her protect her babies.

"This is a Pony Pal Problem," Lulu told her friends. "Let's come up with some ideas."

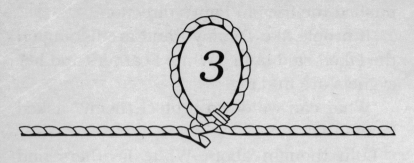

New Friend

Pam put a pile of fries on her plate. "I have an idea," she said. "We should talk to people who fish at the lake. Maybe they don't know that their old fishing line and hooks can hurt birds and animals."

"That's a good idea," agreed Anna.

"We can't talk to everyone," said Lulu. "A lot of people fish very early in the morning or when we're in school."

"We could make a sign," suggested Anna, "and post it at the fishing dock."

Lulu and Pam liked Anna's idea.

"We can also clean up fishing lines and hooks that people leave behind," said Pam.

"If we ride our ponies when we do it," added Lulu, "we can reach the high bushes."

"Brilliant!" exclaimed Anna.

"Let's bring some food for the swans, too," said Pam.

"Maybe the swans will come on shore for it," said Anna. "I'd love to draw them while they eat."

"But we can't get too close to White Feathers," Lulu reminded her friends. "Not until she trusts us."

The girls talked some more about the swans while they finished eating. It was too late for them to go back to the lake that day. They agreed to return in the morning.

The next day, the Pony Pals rode back to Lake Appamapog. Lulu had packed binoculars, her camera, clippers, a collecting bag, five slices of whole wheat bread, a bag of cracked corn, and her Pony Pal whistle. She wore rubber riding boots so she could walk in the water.

Snow White trotted happily along the trail. Snow White wants to see the swans again, too, thought Lulu. When the girls reached the end of Badd Brook, they had their first view of the lake. There were no swans in sight. Lulu scanned the lake and shoreline through her binoculars. "I don't see them," she said.

"We can't see the whole lake from here," Pam reminded Lulu. "I bet they're at the other end."

Lulu hoped Pam was right.

A few minutes later, Pam and Anna rode their ponies into the low water. Lulu waded in, leading Snow White.

Lightning nodded her head as if to say, "This is fun." Acorn nickered cheerfully. Snow White looked around. She's looking for the swans, thought Lulu

Anna and Pam rode along the shoreline and inspected bushes for fishing line.

Lulu studied the bottom of the lake through the ankle-deep water.

"Fishing line is transparent," Lulu told her friends. "It's going to be hard to find it."

Anna was the first to spot fishing line caught in a bush. Pam helped her untangle it.

Snow White pawed the bottom of the lake and whinnied fearfully.

Lulu tightened her grip on the reins and moved closer to her pony. "What's wrong, Snow White?" she asked. Lulu slipped out of the saddle and inspected Snow White's hooves and lower legs. "It's okay," she told her pony. "Everything is okay."

Lulu spoke calmly, but her heart beat fast. She was frightened for her pony. What if she was injured?

Snow White stood still for Lulu, but there was fear in her eyes.

Lulu raised Snow White's right front leg and ran her hand along it. She felt a ridge of thin plastic fishing line. It was loosely

wrapped around Snow White's leg. Lulu took it off and inspected it. Next she checked Snow White's other legs.

"She's okay," Lulu told Pam and Anna. "Some old fishing line was wrapped around her front leg, but there weren't any fish-hooks on it."

Lulu patted Snow White's neck. "You're all right," she said gently. She put the fishing line in her backpack. "You found some fishing line. You're helping."

Lulu tugged a little on Snow White's lead line to move her forward.

Snow White refused to move. Her body trembled.

"She's still scared," observed Anna.

"I'm going to take her out of the water," Lulu said as she turned Snow White toward land. "You keep searching for fishing line. I'll look near the beach."

"Let's signal one another if we see White Feathers and her cygnets," suggested Pam.

"Two long blasts if you see them," said Anna.

"And the SOS signal if there is trouble," added Pam. "Short-long-short."

Lulu agreed to the signals and led Snow White back to land. A few minutes later, they were at the beach. But Snow White was still acting frightened.

Lulu stroked her pony's side. "You're safe," she told her. "You didn't get hurt." Lulu knew singing calmed Snow White, so she sang her pony a lullaby. She gazed into her pony's eyes. They were calm again.

Lulu remembered the first time she sang to Snow White. The pretty white pony was caught in barbed wire that had cut her leg. The fishing line around her leg must have reminded Snow White of the barbed wire, thought Lulu.

Snow White turned toward the lake and nickered. Lulu looked out and saw two cygnets swimming toward them. It was Bottom Up and Friendly. They like the lullaby, too, thought Lulu. Lulu looked in all directions, but she didn't see White Feathers or Slowpoke.

The cygnets are in great danger without their mother, thought Lulu. She took the bread out of the saddlebag, broke it into little pieces, and walked into the water. "Friendly, Bottom Up," she called in a sing-song voice. "Come see what I have for you."

Lulu threw the bread in the cygnets' direction. Bottom Up swam right up to the bread and ate it. Lulu threw another piece, but closer to shore. Friendly swam up to that piece, gulped it down, and looked at Lulu.

"If you want some more," she said as she dropped a small piece of bread on the edge of the sand, "you'll have to come and get it."

Friendly walked over to the bread and ate it. Snow White nickered a hello to him.

Lulu put a piece on the beach. Friendly walked over to it. Bottom Up was still in the water.

Lulu waded farther into the water. "Come on, Bottom Up," she called.

Finally, Bottom Up swam to the sandy edge of the lake. Friendly made a little peeping sound. Bottom Up peeped back to her brother and walked onto land.

Snow White lowered her head and watched the cygnets curiously.

Lulu made a little pen for the cygnets with fallen branches. She was glad that the cygnets were safe. But where is their mother? she wondered. And where's Slow-poke?

Lulu took out her whistle and moved away from the cygnets. She didn't want to frighten them when she blew the SOS signal. But she had to do it. Lulu knew that a mother swan would never leave her young cygnets alone. White Feathers was in trouble.

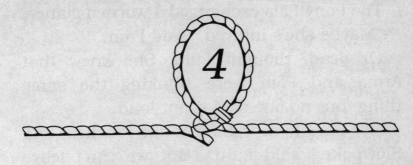

A Plastic Bag

Pam and Anna rode toward Lulu. She waved to them and pointed to the cygnets. The riders slid off their ponies and led them slowly toward the beach.

Lulu met them halfway. Everyone was being careful not to frighten the cygnets.

"Where are White Feathers and Slowpoke?" whispered Pam.

"I don't know," answered Lulu. "Friendly and Bottom Up swam over here alone."

"Do mother swans ever leave their babies alone?" asked Pam.

"No," answered Lulu.

The Pony Pals exchanged a worried glance.

"Maybe she's injured," said Pam.

Or dead, thought Lulu. She knew that Anna and Pam were thinking the same thing, but no one said it out loud.

"We have to search for White Feathers and Slowpoke," said Lulu. "But we can't leave Bottom Up and Friendly alone."

"Lulu, you're the best detective," said Pam. "You should lead the search."

"And you know a lot about injured animals, Pam," said Anna. "So you should go with Lulu. I'll stay here with the cygnets."

"Okay," agreed Pam.

Snow White nickered gently at the cygnets. Friendly tottered closer to the pony and peeped.

"The cygnets like Snow White," observed Anna.

"Can she stay and help me take care of them?" asked Anna. "You can ride Acorn."

"Acorn is the best pony detective," said Pam.

"Besides," added Lulu, "if we wade into the lake, Snow White might spook again."

Anna handed Acorn's reins to Lulu. "I'll signal you if White Feathers and Slowpoke show up here," she said.

"Okay," agreed Lulu as she mounted Acorn.

Pam and Lightning followed Lulu and Acorn onto the lake trail.

"What clues should we look for?" Pam asked Lulu.

"Fresh swan droppings, feathers, and down," answered Lulu. "Down is that white fluffy stuff."

The girls looked for clues as they rode along the trail. Every few minutes, Lulu scanned the lake and shoreline with her binoculars. There was no sign of White Feathers or the smallest cygnet.

They came to a stretch of lakefront with dense bushes and underbrush.

"Acorn and I will search from the water side," Lulu told Pam as she dismounted. "You keep searching on the trail side."

Lulu led Acorn into the shallow water. She scanned the other side of the lake through her binoculars.

Suddenly, Acorn pulled on the reins and whinnied.

"What's wrong, Acorn?" Lulu asked as she turned to the pony.

Acorn stared at a plastic shopping bag caught in the underbrush. Lulu was surprised that Acorn had spooked because of a plastic bag. Usually, nothing spooked Anna's pony.

"It's only a plastic bag," Lulu told Acorn.

Acorn pulled on the reins again and sniffed. He wanted to go closer to the plastic bag. "Okay," Lulu agreed. "You can check it out. But I'm telling you that it's nothing to be afraid of."

When they reached the underbrush, Acorn whinnied softly. Lulu realized that Acorn wasn't spooked and he wasn't interested in the plastic bag. A swan was laying near the bag in the underbrush.

"Pam," Lulu called out, "Acorn found White Feathers."

Lulu moved the plastic bag. She was horrified by what she saw. White Feathers was trapped in fishing line and could not move. Her wings were pinned to her body. A silver fishhook was stuck in her foot and another one was in her leg.

The Pony Pals looked down at the trapped bird.

"Is she alive?" Pam asked in a hoarse whisper.

Before Lulu could answer, White Feathers opened her eyes and looked at them. She seemed to be pleading for help.

"We'll help you, White Feathers," said Pam soothingly.

"How?" Lulu whispered to Pam.

"I don't know," Pam answered. "If we take out the fishhooks, she might start bleeding. If we cut the fishing line, she could swim off with hooks in her leg and foot. The wounds could become infected."

"Should we get your dad?" asked Lulu.

"He doesn't take care of wild animals or birds," answered Pam. "But St. Francis Animal Shelter does. Ms. Raskins has a lot of experience with injured birds."

"I'll find a phone and call the shelter," said Lulu. "You stay here with White Feathers."

"Okay," agreed Pam. "But hurry. I don't know how long White Feathers can last like this."

"I'll be back with help, White Feathers," Lulu told the trapped bird.

As Lulu rode toward the beach, she remembered Slowpoke. They'd found White Feathers, but they hadn't found her smallest cygnet.

Lulu rode off the trail to the paved road. I'll stop at the first house I see, she decided. But she reached the beach before she found a house. Mr. Kline's truck was still parked there. Lulu remembered that Mr. Kline had a cell phone. As she rode toward Anna and Mr. Kline, she blew the SOS signal.

Anna and Mr. Kline saw Lulu and ran to meet her at the hitching post.

"Acorn found White Feathers," Lulu said breathlessly. "She's injured. I need a phone."

Mr. Kline took the cell phone out of his pocket and handed it to Lulu. "I can give you and the swan a ride," he said.

Lulu called directory assistance, asked for the animal shelter number, and waited while it rang. Please answer the phone, Ms. Raskins, Lulu prayed.

Ms. Raskins picked up on the fifth ring.

Lulu quickly told her about the trapped swan and that Mr. Kline and Pam were there to help.

"I can't leave the shelter right now," Ms. Raskins explained. "You need to get that swan to me as quickly as possible. Have Mr. Kline and Pam cut the hooks away from the fishing line. If they can, they should remove them."

"Should we cut the fishing line, too?" asked Lulu. "It's wrapped all around her."

"Don't try to untangle it," cautioned Ms.

Raskins. "It's practically invisible on a swan and very difficult to remove safely. You might strangle her. Just get the hooks out and come as fast as you can. We'll remove the fishing line here."

"Ask her about the cygnets," Anna told Lulu.

Lulu told Ms. Raskins about the cygnets.

"Bring the two you found to the shelter, too," instructed Ms. Raskins.

After Lulu hung up, she spotted a small cardboard box in the back of Mr. Kline's pickup truck. Mr. Kline removed fishing supplies from the box and gave it to Anna. It was the perfect size to carry the cygnets in.

"Pam will help you with the cygnets," Lulu told Anna. "I'll ride in the truck with White Feathers."

"Snow White can come with me and Acorn," said Anna. "I'll hold on to her lead rope."

"You should put the box with the cygnets on Snow White's saddle," suggested Lulu as she climbed into the pickup truck. "And poke breathing holes in the top of the box and put some grass in it."

"Okay," called Anna as Mr. Kline turned on the truck's engine.

Lulu looked back at the two cygnets on the beach. I just hope we're not too late, Lulu prayed. I hope we can save their mother's life.

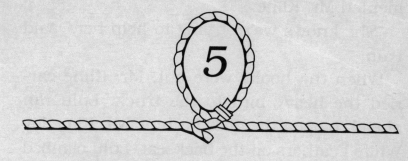

Flashing Red Light

Lulu and Mr. Kline waded through the water toward Pam and White Feathers. "How is she?" asked Lulu.

"She's still breathing," answered Pam.

While Mr. Kline and Pam worked on the swan, Lulu spoke soothingly to her. Pam held back feathers so Mr. Kline could cut the hooks away from the fishing line. Next, Mr. Kline carefully removed the fishhooks. The injured swan didn't move while they worked on her.

"Look how well she's behaving," commented Mr. Kline.

"She knows we're trying to help her," said Pam.

When the hooks were out, Mr. Kline carried the heavy bird to the truck. Lulu ran ahead to open the door for him. Mr. Kline lay White Feathers on the backseat. Lulu climbed in on the other side and sat next to her.

Mr. Kline snapped his volunteer fireman's light to the roof of the truck. It spun around, flashing a red light. "I'll get us there as fast as I can," he told Lulu as he drove onto the road.

Lulu covered White Feathers's trapped wings with her jacket. The swan tucked her head back on her neck and looked at Lulu. She's helpless, frightened, and in pain, thought Lulu.

Lulu reached out and gently touched White Feathers's neck. She hummed a lullaby and gently moved her hand in little circles on the swan's neck. The tiny neck feathers felt lush and soft. White Feathers let out a long, loud sigh. She trusts me, thought Lulu.

Ms. Raskins was waiting for them in front of the shelter's main building. When the truck stopped, she opened the door and looked down at White Feathers.

"Poor swan," she said softly. Ms. Raskins carefully lifted White Feathers out of the truck and carried her over to an examining table. "We don't want to frighten her by bringing her indoors," she explained as she lay White Feathers on the table. "There's a hawk in the examining room."

The table was covered with fresh white paper. A bag of medical supplies was on a chair next to it.

"Can I help you take off the fishing line?" Lulu asked.

"Certainly," answered Ms. Raskins. "I'll need your help."

"I wish I could stay and help, too," said Mr. Kline. "But I have to get back to the store."

Mr. Kline left, and Lulu and Ms. Raskins began White Feathers's treatment.

First, they cleaned the fishhook wounds. "Her wounds are infected," commented Ms. Raskins, "and she's a little feverish."

Next, Ms. Raskins gave White Feathers an antibiotic shot in her chest. Finally, she and Lulu carefully cut and unwrapped the fishing line.

White Feathers seemed to know that they were helping her. She stayed perfectly still the whole time.

When White Feathers's wings were freed, Ms. Raskins felt along the joints. "Nothing seems to be broken," she commented. "Time to put her in the waterfowl pen."

Ms. Raskins put her arms around White Feathers's wings and carried her over to the large pen. Lulu ran ahead and opened the gate for her.

"Okay. Try out your wings," said Ms. Raskins as she set the swan down.

White Feathers stretched her wings, fluffed up her feathers, lifted up her head, and shook herself.

"You'll be okay," Ms. Raskins told White

Feathers. "But you're going to have to stay here for a while."

White Feathers took a few steps forward, but her stride was uneven.

"She's limping," observed Lulu.

"From the infected fishhook wounds," explained Ms. Raskins.

Lulu heard the clip-clop of ponies' hooves. She turned to see her Pony Pals and the three ponies approaching. Anna and Acorn rode first, leading Snow White. The box of cygnets was tied to Snow White's saddle. Pam and Lightning took up the rear. They were headed toward the hitching post behind the building.

"Go meet your friends and tell them to move slowly around White Feathers," Ms. Raskins warned. "She's going to want to protect her babies."

Lulu ran to meet her friends. She told them all the news about White Feathers and Ms. Raskins's warning.

Snow White nuzzled Lulu's shoulder hello. Lulu patted her pony on the head. "Thanks for taking care of Friendly and Bottom Up," she said.

Lulu untied the box of cygnets from Snow White's saddle. Pam and Anna tied the ponies to the hitching post. When Lulu had the box of cygnets in her arms, the Pony Pals walked to the waterfowl pen.

White Feathers didn't see them at first. She was trying out her wings and walking with a limp. Ms. Raskins gave the girls instructions on letting out the cygnets.

Anna opened the gate, and Lulu opened the box and put it on the ground. The little brown swans looked up at her curiously. Lulu lifted out Friendly and placed him inside the gate. Anna took out Bottom Up.

Friendly started peeping.

White Feathers turned and saw her babies. She tossed her head and peeped with excitement as she limped toward them. They ran to her. When the cygnets and White Feathers met, she opened her wings. The babies settled under them.

White Feathers looked around. Lulu won-

dered if she was looking for her missing cygnet.

"How lovely," exclaimed Ms. Raskins.

"Their mother is going to take care of them now," said Anna.

"Actually, I'm going to have to take care of all of them," said Ms. Raskins. "I need to set up a pool, give them food and water, and care for the injured mother." She sighed. "We were understaffed and overworked *before* this family arrived."

"We can help," said the Pony Pals in unison.

"We need to keep an eye on them around the clock for the first twenty-four hours," said Ms. Raskins. "And you have to be very careful around White Feathers. She's injured."

"Is White Feathers going to be okay?" asked Anna.

"Only time will tell," answered Ms. Raskins. "Those wounds are infected and she has a fever. We also have to keep checking her for fishing line. There could still be some wrapped around her legs or neck. That could cut off circulation in her legs or choke her."

"Fishing line is hard to find on a swan," commented Lulu. "They have so many feathers."

"That is exactly the problem," agreed Ms. Raskins.

The Pony Pals watched Friendly and Bottom Up follow their mother around the yard. The mother swan and two of her babies were reunited. But we didn't save Slowpoke, thought Lulu. And White Feathers is still in danger.

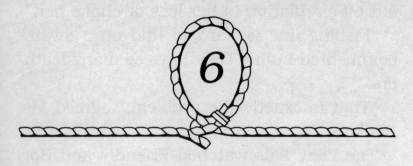

Help Me!

"We'll help you take care of White Feathers and the cygnets," Lulu told Ms. Raskins.

"We can stay overnight," offered Pam. "We've done a lot of night watches for sick ponies."

"We make up a schedule and take turns during the night," explained Lulu.

"We have our own tent and sleeping bags," added Anna.

Ms. Raskins smiled at the Pony Pals. "I can certainly use your help," she said gratefully. "I'll sleep here tonight, too, and take a turn. But you'll have to get permission from your parents."

The girls put the ponies in the paddock and called their homes. Pam's and Anna's parents and Lulu's grandmother all agreed the girls could stay overnight at the shelter. Mrs. Crandal offered to bring them their tent and sleeping bags.

The girls' first job for the swans was to set up a large kiddie swimming pool and fill it with water.

White Feathers watched curiously. When the pool was filled, she limped over and looked in. Her cygnets followed. Ms. Raskins picked up White Feathers and put her in the water. Anna and Lulu put Bottom Up and Friendly near their mother. White Feathers sat in the water and her cygnets climbed on her back.

"That is so sweet," said Anna.

Ms. Raskins smiled at the girls. "Thanks," she said. "You're doing a great job. While they're in the pool, let's clean up the medical supplies and take a break."

During the break Ms. Raskins and the Pony Pals ate cookies, drank juice, and talked about how to care for the swans.

Pam made a list.

TO-DO LIST FOR CARE OF WHITE FEATHERS AND TWO CYGNETS

- **DAILY ANTIBIOTIC INJECTION FOR WHITE FEATHERS**

- **WATCH FOR SIGNS OF MORE FISHING LINE AROUND WHITE FEATHERS'S NECK AND LEGS**
  - Is white Feathers eating okay?
  - Is her foot or leg swollen?

- **CHECK WHITE FEATHERS'S WOUNDS**
  - Is there pus coming from the wound?
  - Does the wound smell bad?
  - Can she walk without limping?

- KEEP THE KIDDIE POOL FILLED WITH FRESH WATER

- PREPARE FOOD
  - wash lettuce and other greens to
  - clean off pesticides.
  - Chop greens for cygnets
  - Nonmedicated bird food for white feathers
  - Make mash of nonmedicated game-bird food and water for cygnets.

- LEAVE OUT FRESH FOOD AND WATER

- CLEAN UP DROPPINGS AND PUT ON COMPOST HEAP

- KEEP PEN VERY CLEAN

The Pony Pals looked over the list. "We should feed them now," said Lulu. Ms. Raskins agreed.

Anna poured fresh water in a big bowl. Lulu and Pam prepared the greens and the mash for the cygnets. Anna put a bowl with bird food on the ground for White Feathers. Meanwhile, Ms. Raskins was feeding the other animals at the shelter.

As the girls were leaving the pen, Mrs. Crandal drove up with their camping gear.

"You watch the swans, Lulu," suggested Pam. "Anna and I will get our gear from my Mom and set up the tent."

Pam and Anna ran toward the truck. Lulu stood outside the pen watching White Feathers and her cygnets eat.

Lulu noticed that White Feathers was eating the cygnets' mash instead of her own food. Has she already finished the bird food? wondered Lulu.

Lulu went into the pen to check the bowl of bird food. White Feathers hadn't eaten any of it. The swan took a nibble of the soft mash. As she swallowed, little choking sounds came from her long neck. It's hard for her to swallow, thought Lulu. Is there still fishing line wrapped around her throat?

"What's wrong, White Feathers?" Lulu asked gently.

The injured swan looked up and walked over to her.

Lulu sat down on the ground. "I want to help you," she said. "Can I look at your neck?"

White Feathers sat in front of Lulu and lay her head and long neck in Lulu's lap. Lulu felt like she was in a dream. White Feathers completely trusted her.

Lulu gently stroked the swan's neck. She worked her fingers deep into the soft feathers. With the tip of her forefinger, she felt a tiny ridge going around the swan's neck.

"Fishing line is choking you," she told White Feathers. "But I found it. Now I have to cut it. Don't move."

The swan stayed still while Lulu felt in her pocket for her camping knife. She took it out

ygnets were on her saddle, she wanted
ay."

e tried to go in the water," added Pam.

d Snow White didn't like the water to-
said Anna. "Remember how she spooked?"

u told her friends that Snow White was
htened in the water because of the day
as caught in barbed wire. "The fishing
round her leg reminded her of that,"
ded Lulu.

t was the day Anna and I met you,"
m.

beginning of the Pony Pals," said

the day we rescued Snow White,"
ulu.

we've rescued White Feathers and
er babies," said Anna.

ot Slowpoke," added Pam sadly.

lost forever," said Anna. "Poor little

ollowed Anna and Pam out of the
and closed the gate behind them.
n't Snow White want to leave the

and opened up the scissors. With the tiny
scissors, Lulu cut the fishing line. Next, she
removed the tangle of line from around the
swan's neck.

White Feathers stretched out her neck and
waggled her tail as if to say, "Thank you."

"You're welcome," said Lulu with a little
bow.

White Feathers limped back to her food.

Lulu looked up and saw her Pony Pals,
Ms. Raskins, and Mrs. Crandal all standing
outside the pen.

Lulu showed them the fishing line and
told them what happened. "White Feathers
put her head in my lap," concluded Lulu. "It
was so beautiful."

"She really trusts you," said Ms. Raskins.

"Lulu has a wonderful way with animals,"
commented Mrs. Crandal.

Anna grinned at Lulu. "Just like your
dad," she said.

I do have a special connection to animals,
thought Lulu. I'll always have them in my
life. Lots of them.

While Ms. Raskins was with the swans, the Pony Pals fed their ponies.

Snow White was standing where she could watch White Feathers and the cygnets. Lulu put her arms around her pony's neck. "They're okay," Lulu told her pony. "We're going to take good care of them."

Snow White sighed.

First there were four swan babies, thought Lulu. Then there were three. Now there are only two. Lulu wished they'd found Slowpoke when they found White Feathers. Was Slowpoke eaten by a turtle or hawk? she wondered. Or was she caught in fishing line like her mother? A little cygnet like that would never survive alone on the lake.

Who was fishing on the lake now? Were they leaving fishing line in the bushes and lake? Would another bird or animal become ensnared?

7

"I Don't Ca

Snow White continued to
When the swans moved t
she followed them with he

"Snow White really lov
and her babies," Lulu tol
think she'd follow them

"That's why I was sur
she gave Acorn a handf

"Surprised by what?"

"Snow White didn'
beach with us," answe

the
to st
"S
"A
day,"
Lul
so fri
she w
line a
conclu
"Tha
said P
"The
Anna.
"And
added I
"Now
two of h
"But r
"She's
thing."
Lulu f
paddock
"Why did

lake with Bottom Up and Friendly?" she wondered out loud.

Anna turned to Lulu. "Maybe she wanted to stay because of Slowpoke," she said. "Maybe Snow White thinks Slowpoke is still alive."

"Ponies can smell and hear things people can't," said Pam.

"Snow White might have smelled Slowpoke," said Lulu. "Or maybe she heard her peeping!"

"How could she be alive?" asked Anna. "There are lots of turtles in that lake. It's so dangerous out there for one little cygnet."

"I don't know," answered Lulu. "But we have to go back and search for her."

"You're right," agreed Pam.

Lulu told Ms. Raskins their plan.

"It is *possible* a lone cygnet could still be alive," Ms. Raskins admitted. "But it's unlikely. And it will be so difficult to find a little brown creature in that big lake."

"We want to try," said Anna. "Snow White will help."

"I'll watch the swans while you're gone," Ms. Raskins said. She looked at the sky. "The sun will be setting in two hours. You shouldn't ride after dark."

The Pony Pals promised that they would return before sunset.

"Hurry," Lulu shouted to her friends as she ran back to the paddock. "We don't have much time."

Lulu put Snow White's saddle back on. "We're going to the lake again," she explained to her pony. "We're going to look for Slowpoke."

Pam led for the first part of the ride.

When they reached the lake trail, Lulu took the lead. A hawk flew overhead. Did that hawk eat Slowpoke? wondered Lulu.

Lulu turned in the saddle. "We'll start the search at the beach where we found the other cygnets," she called to her friends.

Lulu was the first to see Mike and Tommy fishing from the dock. She pointed them out to Anna and Pam as they continued toward the beach.

The boys finally noticed them.

"The Pony Pests are everywhere," shouted Tommy. He turned to Mike. "Call the exterminator!"

Anna and Lulu exchanged a glance. Anna rolled her eyes. Tommy always made the same stupid, not-very-funny exterminator joke about the "Pony Pests."

The three girls halted their ponies beside the dock.

Tommy glared at them. "You can't fish on this dock," he said. "We were here first."

"You don't own this lake, Tommy Rand," Anna scolded. "Or the dock."

" 'You don't own this lake, Tommy Rand,' " he repeated in a high-pitched voice. " 'Or the dock.' "

"Don't start that, Tommy," said Anna. "And don't copy what I just said."

Tommy ignored Anna and repeated *exactly* what she had said.

Anna clamped her mouth shut and glared at him.

Lulu turned to Mike. "Remember the big white swan?" she asked.

"Yeah," answered Mike.

"She got caught up in old fishing line," she said. "That swan almost died. She's at St. Francis Animal Shelter. She could still die."

Mike looked concerned. "That's awful," he said. "What about the baby swans? What happened to them?"

Lulu started to tell Mike how they rescued two of the cygnets, when Tommy interrupted.

"What do you care about a dumb old bird?" he asked Mike.

"We've got to be more careful with our fishing line," Mike told him.

"You be careful," snarled Tommy. "I'll be fishing."

Tommy turned his back on Mike and the Pony Pals and threw out his line.

Snow White tugged on the reins and nickered nervously. Snow White doesn't like being around fishing line, thought Lulu. It's spooking her. She backed her pony away from the dock.

"Please don't leave fishing line in the lake

or bushes," Pam told Mike. "It can kill birds and animals."

"Mr. Kline is recycling old fishing line at the hardware store," added Lulu. "You can bring it there."

"Tell Rosalie there are swans she can visit at the shelter, Mike," Anna said. "The cygnets are really cute."

Rosalie was Mike's younger sister. She called herself a Junior Pony Pal, but she didn't have a pony. Rosalie loved ponies, especially Acorn.

"Yeah, sure," he agreed.

"Mike, the problem with the fishing line is serious," added Pam.

"I know," Mike said in a low voice.

"Hey, man," Tommy called over his shoulder to Mike. "You fishing or turning into a Pony Pest?"

Mike quickly turned from the Pony Pals, picked up his fishing rod, and walked back to Tommy.

"We're wasting our time with these guys," said Pam.

We weren't wasting our time on Mike, thought Lulu. He cares about the swans and he'll be more careful with his fishing line now.

She looked at her watch. They only had an hour to search for Slowpoke. Will we find her? she wondered. And if we do, will she be dead or alive?

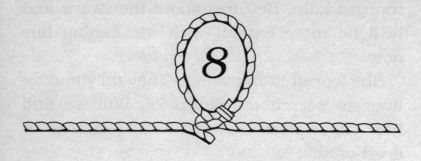

A Bump on a Log

The girls rode to the spot where Friendly and Bottom Up came on shore.

Anna looked over the big lake and densely wooded waterfront. "How do we look for her?" she asked.

"I'll walk in the water and lead Snow White," said Lulu.

"We don't have rubber riding boots," said Pam. "So we'll ride."

Lulu dismounted and led Snow White on a loose lead. Snow White walked into the water ahead of her.

The Pony Pals exchanged a surprised look.

"I'm going to follow her," said Lulu as she waded into the water behind her pony. Anna and Pam followed on their ponies.

Snow White walked slowly along the edge of the lake. She stopped twice and sniffed. The third time she stopped, her ears went forward. She whinnied softly.

"She's listening to something," whispered Lulu.

Snow White walked over to a dead tree. It hung a few inches above the water and was covered with vines. Lulu inspected the water and brambles under the tree trunk. There was no sign of the cygnet.

"I guess it was a false lead," said Lulu. She grabbed Snow White's halter and tried to turn her around. Snow White shook her head. She didn't want to leave.

"I think I see her," said Anna excitedly. "Look on that log."

Lulu studied the bumpy tree trunk. She didn't see the cygnet. Then one of the "bumps" near the water moved. Lulu waded over to the "bump." It was the little cygnet.

"Slowpoke," she said in a hushed voice.

Anna slid off Acorn and stood ankle-deep in the water. Pam dismounted, too.

"She's caught in the vines," said Anna.

"Maybe she was trying to hide and she couldn't get out," said Pam.

The little cygnet peeped pitifully.

"I'll hold Slowpoke and you free her," Lulu told Anna and Pam.

Lulu put her hands gently around the tiny bird. Her feathers felt downy and soft. Her body trembled.

"Don't be afraid," Lulu said gently. "We're going to bring you to your mother."

"She must be so hungry," said Anna.

"And thirsty," added Pam as she cut the vine. "She can't reach the water from here."

Lulu gently placed Slowpoke in the water. The weak little cygnet drank.

Pam pulled grass up from the shore, tore it into little pieces, and put them on the water. Slowpoke ate a few small pieces.

"I don't think she's injured," said Pam.

added Pam. "But otherwise, we think she's okay."

Ms. Raskins looked the cygnet over while the Pony Pals tied their ponies to the hitching post. "Poor little thing," she said. "She seems very weak." She handed Slowpoke to Lulu. "You bring her to her mother."

Lulu carefully carried the tiny cygnet over to the waterfowl pen.

"I have a surprise for you," she said as she went through the gate. She put Slowpoke on the ground. The little cygnet peeped.

White Feathers's head popped up and she looked around. When she saw Slowpoke she honked for her. Slowpoke ran under her mother's wing. The other two cygnets joined her.

"Good work, girls," said Ms. Raskins. "You rescued White Feathers and her missing cygnet."

"Snow White is the one who found the cygnet," said Anna.

"And Acorn found White Feathers," added Lulu.

Pam looked over at the swans. "White Feathers is still limping," she observed.

"Is she going to be okay?" asked Anna.

"Her wound is infected," answered Ms. Raskins. "If the infection spreads, it can be very dangerous."

Lulu watched White Feathers with her babies under her wings. If she dies, thought Lulu, her three cygnets will be orphans.

Visitors

The girls unsaddled their ponies and put them in the paddock again. Meanwhile, Ms. Raskins put out a picnic supper.

Before they ate, the girls and Ms. Raskins made a schedule for watching the swans.

"I'll watch from four A.M. to six A.M.," volunteered Ms. Raskins.

Pam wrote it down. The Pony Pals divided up the rest of the night hours.

While they ate supper, Ms. Raskins told them interesting stories about rescuing animals.

After dinner, Ms. Raskins went to her office to do paperwork. The Pony Pals began their turns watching the swans. Anna and Lulu kept Pam company during her shift. But soon Lulu was yawning.

"You two get some sleep," said Pam. "I'll wake you when it's your turn, Anna."

Lulu fell asleep a few seconds after she lay down. The next thing she knew, someone was calling her name.

"Wake up, Lulu," a voice whispered.

Lulu rolled over in her sleeping bag and opened her eyes.

Anna was kneeling beside her. "It's two o'clock," she said. "Your turn to watch the swans."

Lulu unzipped her sleeping bag and sat up. "How's White Feathers?" she asked in a low voice.

"She woke up and drank a lot of water," Anna answered as she handed Lulu the flashlight. "Her wound looks a little red."

Lulu crawled out of the tent and zipped the flap closed behind her. A three-quarter moon glowed in the star-studded sky. She looked into the shed. White Feathers's neck and head were resting on her back. The cygnets were asleep under her wings. Lulu was happy to see White Feathers resting, but worried about her infection.

Next, she went over the To-Do list. There was plenty of fresh food and water in the pen. She shoveled up swan droppings and put them on the compost heap. "That's done," she said to herself as she sat under a tree.

Lulu leaned against the tree trunk and thought about the swans. So much had happened in a short time. She remembered it all like a movie in her mind: a movie with scary parts and happy ones. She hoped White Feathers would get better and her mind-movie would have a happy ending.

The next morning the Pony Pals and Ms. Raskins checked White Feathers carefully. There was no pus in her wounds and they didn't smell bad anymore. Her foot wasn't very swollen and she was limping less.

"She seems to be recovering," Ms. Raskins said as she gave White Feathers her daily antibiotic shot. "And Slowpoke is in good shape."

Lulu looked over at the littlest cygnet. She spent more time eating than her brother and sister.

"Can they ever go back to the lake?" asked Anna.

Ms. Raskins smiled at the girls and nodded. "If White Feathers continues to recover," she said, "they can go back on Saturday."

"Great!" exclaimed Pam.

"I hope they'll be safe at the lake," said Anna.

"Let's work on our sign," suggested Pam. "That will help keep them safe."

"We can make it here," said Lulu, "so we can help take care of the swans while we work."

The girls went over to the picnic table to have a Pony Pal meeting about the sign.

Anna opened the meeting. "The first thing we have to do is make a list of supplies," she said.

"Then we have to decide what the sign is going to say," put in Pam.

"And how it will look," added Lulu. She smiled at Anna. "Let's have pictures of the swans and other wildlife on it."

"Okay," agreed Anna. "That'll be fun to do." She reached into her backpack and took out her sketch pad and pencil case.

Pam handed Lulu her little pocket notebook. "Here," she said. "You make the list of supplies we'll need."

"The first thing we need is a big piece of wood," said Anna.

Lulu wrote it down.

"And house paint," added Pam.

"What colors should we get, Anna?" asked Lulu.

Anna looked up from her sketchbook. She was already practicing drawing swans. "We need primary colors," she answered. "Red, yellow, and blue. I can mix anything from those. It would be great to have some black and white, too."

ʼlu added the five paint colors to her list.

"And we'll need a few brushes," said Anna, "in different sizes."

Lulu wrote *Brushes* on the list.

"We can get all those supplies at the hardware store," commented Pam. "But it's going to cost a lot of money."

"Maybe Mr. Kline will donate some of it," said Lulu. "It's for a good cause."

"I bet he will," agreed Pam. "He was upset about what happened to White Feathers."

The girls were in the middle of their meeting when Mike, Rosalie, and Rosalie's friend Mimi came to the shelter. Lulu ran over to meet them. "Don't make any big noises around the mother swan," she warned. "And don't get too close."

Mimi hugged Lulu around the waist. "I love swans," she said. "I think they're the prettiest birds. Rosalie does, too."

"Where are the swans?" asked Rosalie. "Where's Ms. Raskins?"

"She's in her office," answered Lulu. "Go tell her you're here and she'll show you the swans. Okay?"

"Okay," agreed Rosalie.

The two younger girls ran off, but Mike stayed with Lulu.

"Is the mother swan okay?" he asked.

"She's getting better," Lulu told him.

He looked in the direction of the picnic table. Anna was drawing and Pam was writing.

"What are you guys doing?" he asked. "Making a report on swans?"

Lulu told him about the sign. She headed back to the table. Mike walked beside her, but looked toward the waterfowl pen.

"Hey, there's the third cygnet," he said. "You found her!"

"Snow White did," she said.

Mike smiled. Lulu could see that he was really happy that they had rescued Slowpoke.

When they reached the table, Anna looked up at Mike. "Where's your bad-boy buddy?" she asked.

"Stop saying Tommy's bad," said Mike.

"You just don't know him like I do. He's a great guy."

Lulu and Anna exchanged a glance. They hated it when Mike defended Tommy. As Lulu sat down next to Pam, she thought about how White Feathers's mate died.

"Does Tommy have a bow and arrow?" she asked Mike.

"Yeah," he answered. "So what?"

"*So*," said Lulu, "the father of those baby swans was killed by a bow and arrow. Maybe your wonderful Tommy Rand did that!"

Mike's face turned pale. "Tommy wouldn't hurt a swan," he protested.

"Are you sure?" asked Lulu.

Home, Sweet Home

Mike looked sad and confused. "Tommy just got the bow and arrow on Saturday," Mike said. "He doesn't even know how to use it that good."

Lulu tapped her pencil on the table and thought. She realized that Tommy Rand probably didn't kill White Feathers's mate.

"I just don't think he'd hurt a swan," insisted Mike.

"You're right, Mike," Lulu admitted. "The swan was shot *before* Tommy had a bow and arrow."

WHITE FEATHERS FRIENDLY

BOTTOM UP

SLOW POKE

The next morning, the Pony Pals rode to the shelter. When White Feathers saw them, she spread her wings.

"I think she knows that this is a special day," said Anna.

The girls tied their ponies to the hitching post and checked the sign. Lulu gently touched it in several places. "It's totally dry," she announced.

"Put it in the back of the van," Ms. Raskins directed. "Then we'll pack up our swan family.

Pam opened the big carrier

Mike's sad look turned into a smile. "I told you Tommy's not a bad guy," he said with relief.

"Yeah, right!" Pam snapped.

Lulu just shook her head.

Anna rolled her eyes.

Rosalie and Mimi ran over to the table.

"We saw the swans. We saw the swans," chanted Mimi. She climbed up on the table and sat facing Anna.

"They're so cute," said Rosalie as she sat down next to Lulu.

Ms. Raskins followed the girls to the table. She said hello to Mike and thanked him for bringing Rosalie and Mimi.

"Rosalie and Mimi would like to watch when the swans go back to the lake," Ms. Raskins said. "Maybe you could bring them, Mike. We'll do it at noon on Saturday."

"Sure," agreed Mike.

"We'll tell Mr. Kline, too," put in Anna. "We have to go to the hardware store later."

"That's my hardware store," Mimi said proudly.

"Only because your mom and dad own it," said Rosalie.

"I know," said Mimi.

Later that day the Pony Pals rode over to the hardware store.

Mr. Kline was pleased to see the girls and their ponies. They told him about saving Slowpoke. They also asked him to donate supplies for the sign. He donated all the wood, paint, and brushes.

"I'll deliver it to the shelter after work," he promised.

For the next three days, the girls went to the shelter. They worked on the sign and helped take care of the swans. Each day White Feathers was a little better. Each day the Pony Pals went for a trail ride to exercise their ponies.

Friday, at noon, the sign was finally finished.

The girls stood back to admire it.

HOW TO PROTECT WILDLIFE AT LAKE APPAMAPOG

DON'Ts

- DON'T leave any fishing line at the lake
- DON'T use lead weights on fishing lures
- DON'T frighten birds with quick or loud noises
- DON'T feed birds moldy or white bread
- DON'T litter

DO's

- DO recycle fishing line by bringing it to Kline's Hardware Store
- DO keep a safe distance from swans
- DO report any injured birds to St. Francis Animal Shelter
- DO keep dogs away from birds
- DO sing to swans
- DO enjoy our beautiful sw

Feathers. Lulu got the box for the cygnets. While Ms. Raskins picked up White Feathers, the Pony Pals each picked up a cygnet. They carefully placed the swans in their containers. Next, the carrier and box were safely packed into the van.

"It's time for White Feathers and her cygnets to go home," announced Ms. Raskins as she got into the van. "We'll meet you at the beach."

The girls remounted their ponies.

Snow White whinnied as if to ask, "What's going on?"

"White Feathers and her babies are going back to the lake," Lulu told her.

When the Pony Pals reached the beach, Ms. Raskins was already there. So were Mimi, Rosalie, Mike, and Mr. Kline. Mike was helping Mr. Kline put up the sign.

Pam and Ms. Raskins took the carrier with White Feathers. Lulu carried the box of cygnets. They put them on the edge of the sand and opened them up. Ms. Raskins lifted out White Feathers. Pam took out

Friendly, Lulu took out Bottom Up, and Anna was responsible for Slowpoke.

They placed the swan and her cygnets at the water's edge.

White Feathers slowly waddled into the water. Her cygnets tottered after her. The white swan paused for a few seconds, then swam slowly out onto the lake. Her cygnets swam behind her.

Snow White whinnied in their direction as if to say, "Hey, where are you going?"

White Feathers turned in the water, rose up on her tail, and spread her wings. Everyone on the shore clapped.

Anna waved. "Bye, White Feathers," she called. "We'll see you around."

"Good luck," shouted Lulu.

"We'll be watching out for you," called Pam.

Friendly spread out his little wings just like his mother. Bottom Up dived for food. Slowpoke tried to keep up with her mother and siblings.

Lulu noticed a few brown feathers near her feet. She picked them up.

"I'll be right back," Lulu told her friends.

Lulu went over to the hitching post and put the small feathers in Snow White's halter. Snow White nuzzled Lulu's shoulder. "The feathers are a present from your friends," she whispered to her pony.

Lulu and Snow White stood side by side, watching the swans. Lulu began to hum "Row, Row, Row Your Boat." Anna and Pam joined in. Rosalie and Mimi did, too. Then Mike and Ms. Raskins added their voices.

White Feathers raised her wings one more time. Snow White sighed contentedly.

Lulu put an arm around Snow White's neck and the other arm around Acorn's. "Thank you," she told the ponies. "Thank you for saving the swans."